Edison's Conquest of Mars

Garrett Putman Serviss

Alpha Editions

This edition published in 2021

ISBN : 9789354599484

Design and Setting By
Alpha Editions
www.alphaedis.com
Email - info@alphaedis.com

As per information held with us this book is in Public Domain.
This book is a reproduction of an important historical work. Alpha Editions uses the best technology to reproduce historical work in the same manner it was first published to preserve its original nature. Any marks or number seen are left intentionally to preserve its true form.

Contents

Chapter I	- 1 -
Chapter II	- 10 -
Chapter III	- 20 -
Chapter IV	- 34 -
Chapter V	- 42 -
Chapter VI	- 58 -
Chapter VII	- 72 -
Chapter VIII	- 90 -
Chapter IX	- 104 -
Chapter X	- 119 -
Chapter XI	- 136 -
Chapter XII	- 146 -
Chapter XIII	- 158 -
Chapter XIV	- 173 -
Chapter XV	- 184 -
Chapter XVI	- 197 -
Chapter XVII	- 209 -
Chapter XVIII	- 217 -

Chapter I

It is impossible that the stupendous events which followed the disastrous invasion of the earth by the Martians should go without record, and circumstances having placed the facts at my disposal, I deem it a duty, both to posterity and to those who were witnesses of and participants in the avenging counterstroke that the earth dealt back at its ruthless enemy in the heavens, to write down the story in a connected form.

The Martians had nearly all perished, not through our puny efforts, but in consequence of disease, and the few survivors fled in one of their projectile cars, inflicting their cruelest blow in the act of departure.

Their Mysterious Explosive.

They possessed a mysterious explosive, of unimaginable puissance, with whose aid they set their car in motion for Mars from a point in Bergen County, N. J., just back of the Palisades.

The force of the explosion may be imagined when it is recollected that they had to give the car a velocity of more than seven miles per second in order to overcome the attraction of the earth and the resistance of the atmosphere.

The shock destroyed all of New York that had not already fallen a prey, and all the buildings yet standing in the surrounding towns and cities fell in one far-circling ruin.

The Palisades tumbled in vast sheets, starting a tidal wave in the Hudson that drowned the opposite shore.

Thousands of Victims.

The victims of this ferocious explosion were numbered by tens of thousands, and the shock, transmitted through the rocky frame of the globe, was recorded by seismographic pendulums in England and on the Continent of Europe.

The terrible results achieved by the invaders had produced everywhere a mingled feeling of consternation and hopelessness. The devastation was widespread. The death-dealing engines which the Martians had brought with them had proved irresistible and the inhabitants of the earth possessed nothing capable of contending against them. There had been no protection for the great cities; no protection even for the open country. Everything had gone down before the savage onslaught of those merciless invaders from space. Savage ruins covered the sites of many formerly flourishing towns and villages, and the broken walls of great cities stared at the heavens like the exhumed skeletons of Pompeii. The awful agencies had extirpated pastures and meadows and dried up the very springs of fertility in the earth where they had touched it. In some parts of the devastated lands pestilence broke out; elsewhere there was famine. Despondency black as night brooded over some of the fairest portions of the globe.

All Not Yet Destroyed.

Yet all had not been destroyed, because all had not been reached by the withering hand of the destroyer. The Martians had not had time to complete their work before they themselves fell a prey to the diseases that carried them off at the very culmination of their triumph.

From those lands which had, fortunately, escaped invasion, relief was sent to the sufferers. The outburst of pity and of charity exceeded anything that the world had known. Differences of race and religion were swallowed up in the universal sympathy which was felt for those who had suffered so terribly from an evil that was as unexpected as it was unimaginable in its enormity.

But the worst was not yet. More dreadful than the actual suffering and the scenes of death and devastation which overspread the afflicted lands was the profound mental and moral depression that followed. This was shared even by those who had not seen the Martians and had not witnessed the destructive effects of the frightful engines of war that they had imported for the conquest of the earth. All mankind was sunk deep in this universal despair, and it became tenfold blacker when the astronomers announced from their observatories that strange lights were visible, moving and flashing upon the red surface of the Planet of War. These mysterious appearances could only be interpreted in the light of past experience to mean that the Martians were preparing for another invasion of the earth, and who could doubt that with the invincible powers of destruction at their command they would this time make their work complete and final?

A Startling Announcement.

This startling announcement was the more pitiable in its effects because it served to unnerve and discourage those few of stouter hearts and more hopeful temperaments who had already begun the labor of restoration and reconstruction amid the embers of their desolated homes. In New York this feeling of hope and confidence, this determination to rise against disaster and to wipe out the evidences of its dreadful presence as quickly as possible, had especially manifested itself. Already a company had been formed and a large amount of capital subscribed for the reconstruction of the destroyed bridges over the East River. Already architects were busily at work planning new twenty-story hotels and apartment houses; new churches and new cathedrals on a grander scale than before.

The Martians Returning.

Amid this stir of renewed life came the fatal news that Mars was undoubtedly preparing to deal us a death blow. The sudden revulsion of feeling flitted like the shadow of an eclipse over the earth. The scenes that followed were indescribable. Men lost their reason. The faint-hearted ended the suspense with self-destruction, the stout-hearted remained steadfast, but without hope and knowing not what to do.

But there was a gleam of hope of which the general public as yet knew nothing. It was due to a few dauntless men of science, conspicuous among whom were Lord Kelvin, the great English savant, Herr Roentgen, the discoverer of the famous X ray, and especially Thomas A. Edison, the American genius of science. These men and a few others had examined with the utmost care the engines of war, the flying machines, the generators of mysterious destructive forces that the Martians had produced, with the object of discovering, if possible, the sources of their power.

Suddenly from Mr. Edison's laboratory at Orange flashed the startling intelligence that he had not only discovered the manner in which the invaders had been able to produce the mighty energies which they employed with such terrible effect, but that, going further, he had found a way to overcome them.

The glad news was quickly circulated throughout the civilized world. Luckily the Atlantic cables had not been destroyed by the Martians, so that communication between the Eastern and Western continents was uninterrupted. It was a proud day for America. Even while the Martians had been upon the earth, carrying everything before them, demonstrating to the confusion of the most optimistic that there was no possibility of standing against them, a feeling—a confidence had manifested itself in France, to a minor extent in England, and particularly in Russia, that the Americans might discover means to meet and master the invaders.

Now, it seemed, this hope and expectation were to be realized. Too late, it is true, in a certain sense, but not too late to meet the new invasion which the astronomers had announced was impending. The effect was as wonderful and indescribable as that of the despondency which but a little while before had overspread the world. One could almost hear the universal sigh of relief which went up from humanity. To relief succeeded confidence—so quickly does the human spirit recover like an elastic spring, when pressure is released.

"We Are Ready for Them!"

"Let them come," was the almost joyous cry. "We shall be ready for them now. The Americans have solved the problem. Edison has placed the means of victory within our power."

Looking back upon that time now, I recall, with a thrill, the pride that stirred me at the thought that, after all, the inhabitants of the Earth were a match for those terrible men from Mars, despite all the advantage which they had gained from their millions of years of prior civilization and science.

As good fortunes, like bad, never come singly, the news of Mr. Edison's discovery was quickly followed by additional glad tidings from that laboratory of marvels in the lap of the Orange mountains. During their career of conquest the Martians had astonished the inhabitants of the earth no less with their flying machines—which navigated our atmosphere as easily as they had that of their native planet—than with their more destructive inventions. These flying machines in themselves had given them an enormous advantage in the contest. High above the desolation that they had caused to reign on the surface of the earth, and, out of the range of our guns, they had hung safe in the upper air. From the clouds they had dropped death upon the earth.

Edison's Flying Machine.

Now, rumor declared that Mr. Edison had invented and perfected a flying machine much more complete and manageable than those of the Martians had been. Wonderful stories quickly found their way into the newspapers concerning what Mr. Edison had already accomplished with the aid of his model electrical balloon. His laboratory was carefully guarded against the invasion of the curious, because he rightly felt that a premature announcement, which should promise more than could be actually fulfilled, would, at this critical juncture, plunge mankind back again into the gulf of despair, out of which it had just begun to emerge.

Nevertheless, inklings of the truth leaked out. The flying machine had been seen by many persons hovering by night high above the Orange hills and disappearing in the faint starlight as if it had gone away into the depths of space, out of which it would re-emerge before the morning light had streaked the east, and be seen settling down again within the walls that surrounded the laboratory of the great inventor. At length the rumor, gradually deepening into a conviction, spread that Edison himself, accompanied by a few scientific friends, had made an experimental trip to the moon. At a time when the spirit of mankind was less profoundly stirred, such a story would have been received with complete incredulity, but now, rising on the wings of the new hope that was buoying up the earth, this extraordinary rumor became a day star of truth to the nations.

Edison's Wonderful Invention Appears.

The flying machine had been seen by many persons, hovering by night high above the Orange Hills and disappearing in the faint starlight.

A Trip to the Moon.

And it was true. I had myself been one of the occupants of the car of the flying Ship of Space on that night when it silently left the earth, and rising out of the great shadow of the globe, sped on to the moon. We had landed upon the scarred and desolate face of the earth's satellite, and but that there are greater and more interesting events, the telling of which must not be delayed, I should undertake to describe the particulars of this first visit of men to another world.

But, as I have already intimated, this was only an experimental trip. By visiting this little nearby island in the ocean of space, Mr. Edison simply wished to demonstrate the practicability of his invention, and to convince, first of all, himself and his scientific friends that it was possible for men—mortal men—to quit and to revisit the earth at their will. That aim this experimental trip triumphantly attained.

The Trial Trip To The Moon.

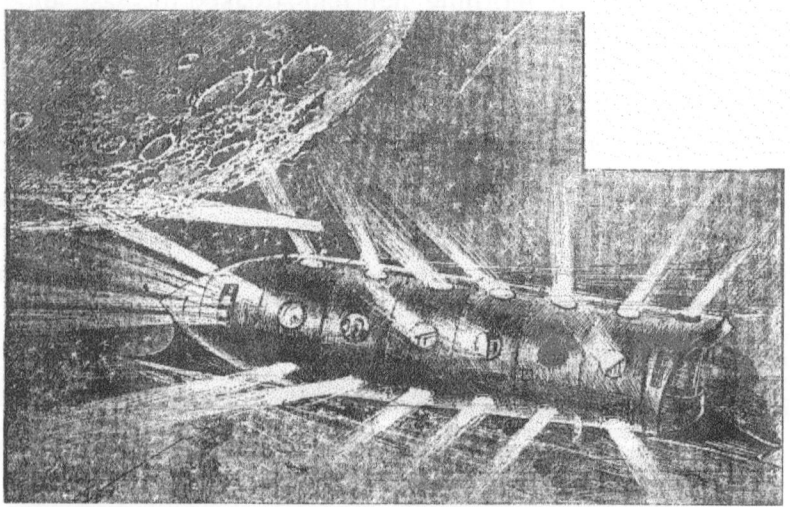

I had myself been one of the occupants of the car of the flying Ship of Space on that night, when it silently left the earth, and rising out of the great shadow of the globe, sped on to the moon.

It would carry me into technical details that would hardly interest the reader to describe the mechanism of Mr. Edison's flying machine. Let it suffice to say that it depended upon the principal of electrical attraction and repulsion. By means of a most ingenious and complicated construction he had mastered the problem of how to produce, in a limited space, electricity of any desired potential and of any polarity, and that without danger to the experimenter or to the material experimented upon. It is gravitation, as everybody knows, that makes man a prisoner on the earth. If he could overcome, or neutralize, gravitation he could float away a free creature of interstellar space. Mr. Edison in his invention had pitted electricity against gravitation. Nature, in fact, had done the same thing long before. Every astronomer knew it, but none had been able to imitate or to reproduce this miracle of nature. When a comet approaches the sun, the orbit in which it travels indicates that it is moving under the impulse of the sun's gravitation. It is in reality falling in a great parabolic or elliptical curve through space. But, while a comet approaches the sun it begins to display—stretching out for millions, and sometimes hundreds of millions of miles on the side away from the sun—an immense luminous train called its tail. This train extends back into that part of space from which the comet is moving. Thus the sun at one and the same time is drawing the comet toward itself and driving off from the comet in an opposite direction minute particles or atoms which, instead of obeying the gravitational force, are plainly compelled to disobey it. That this energy, which the sun exercises against its own gravitation, is electrical in its nature, hardly anybody will doubt. The head of the comet being comparatively heavy and massive, falls on toward the sun, despite the electrical repulsion. But the atoms which form the tail, being almost without weight, yield to the electrical rather than to the gravitational influence, and so fly away from the sun.

Gravity Overcome.

Now, what Mr. Edison had done was, in effect, to create an electrified particle which might be compared to one of the atoms composing the tail of a comet, although in reality it was a kind of car, of metal, weighing some hundreds of pounds and capable of bearing some thousands of pounds with it in its flight. By producing, with the aid of the electrical generator contained in this car, an enormous charge of electricity, Mr. Edison was able to counterbalance, and a trifle more than counterbalance, the attraction of the earth, and thus cause the car to fly off from the earth as an electrified pithball flies from the prime conductor.

As we sat in the brilliantly lighted chamber that formed the interior of the car, and where stores of compressed air had been provided together with chemical apparatus, by means of which fresh supplies of oxygen and nitrogen might be obtained for our consumption during the flight through space, Mr. Edison touched a polished button, thus causing the generation of the required electrical charge on the exterior of the car, and immediately we began to rise.

The moment and direction of our flight had been so timed and prearranged, that the original impulse would carry us straight toward the moon.

A Triumphant Test.

When we fell within the sphere of attraction of that orb it only became necessary to so manipulate the electrical charge upon our car as nearly, but not quite, to counterbalance the effect of the moon's attraction in order that we might gradually approach it and with an easy motion, settle, without shock, upon its surface.

We did not remain to examine the wonders of the moon, although we could not fail to observe many curious things therein. Having demonstrated the fact that we could not only leave the earth, but could journey through space and safely land upon the surface of another planet, Mr. Edison's immediate purpose was fulfilled, and we hastened back to the earth, employing in leaving the moon and landing again upon our own planet the same means of control over the electrical attraction and repulsion between the respective planets and our car which I have already described.

Telegraphing the News.

When actual experiment had thus demonstrated the practicability of the invention, Mr. Edison no longer withheld the news of what he had been doing from the world. The telegraph lines and the ocean cables labored with the messages that in endless succession, and burdened with an infinity of detail, were sent all over the earth. Everywhere the utmost enthusiasm was aroused.

"Let the Martians come," was the cry. "If necessary, we can quit the earth as the Athenians fled from Athens before the advancing host of Xerxes, and like them, take refuge upon our ships—these new ships of space, with which American inventiveness has furnished us."

And then, like a flash, some genius struck out an idea that fired the world.

"Why should we wait? Why should we run the risk of having our cities destroyed and our lands desolated a second time? Let us go to Mars. We have the means. Let us beard the lion in his den. Let us ourselves turn conquerors and take possession of that detestable planet, and if necessary, destroy it in order to relieve the earth of this perpetual threat which now hangs over us like the sword of Damocles."

The Wizard and the Astronomer Confer.

A consultation in Wizard Edison's laboratory between him and Professor Serviss on the best means of repaying the damage wrought upon this planet by the Martians.

Chapter II

This enthusiasm would have had but little justification had Mr. Edison done nothing more than invent a machine which could navigate the atmosphere and the regions of interplanetary space.

He had, however, and this fact was generally known, although the details had not yet leaked out—invented also machines of war intended to meet the utmost that the Martians could do for either offence or defence in the struggle which was now about to ensue.

A Wonderful Instrument.

Acting upon the hint which had been conveyed from various investigations in the domain of physics, and concentrating upon the problem all those unmatched powers of intellect which distinguished him, the great inventor had succeeded in producing a little implement which one could carry in his hand, but which was more powerful than any battleship that ever floated. The details of its mechanism could not be easily explained, without the use of tedious technicalities and the employment of terms, diagrams and mathematical statements, all of which would lie outside the scope of this narrative. But the principle of the thing was simple enough. It was upon the great scientific doctrine, which we have since seen so completely and brilliantly developed, of the law of harmonic vibrations, extending from atoms and molecules at one end of the series up to worlds and suns at the other end, that Mr. Edison based his invention.

Every kind of substance has its own vibratory rhythm. That of iron differs from that of pine wood. The atoms of gold do not vibrate in the same time or through the same range as those of lead, and so on for all known substances, and all the chemical elements. So, on a larger scale, every massive body has its period of vibration. A great suspension bridge vibrates, under the impulse of forces that are applied to it, in long periods. No company of soldiers ever crosses such a bridge without breaking step. If they tramped together, and were followed by other companies keeping the same time with their feet, after a while the vibrations of the bridge would become so great and destructive that it would fall in pieces. So any structure, if its vibration rate is known, could easily be destroyed by a force applied to it in such a way that it should simply increase the swing of those vibrations up to the point of destruction.

Now Mr. Edison had been able to ascertain the vibratory swing of many well-known substances, and to produce, by means of the instrument which he had contrived, pulsations in the ether which were completely under his control, and which could be made long or short, quick or slow, at his will. He could run through the whole gamut from the slow vibrations of sound in air up to the four hundred and twenty-five millions of millions of vibrations per second of the ultra red rays.

Having obtained an instrument of such power, it only remained to concentrate its energy upon a given object in order that the atoms composing that object should be set into violent undulation, sufficient to burst it asunder and to scatter its molecules broadcast. This the inventor effected by the simplest means in the world—simply a parabolic reflector by which the destructive waves could be sent like a beam of light, but invisible, in any direction and focused upon any desired point.

Testing the "Disintegrator."

I had the good fortune to be present when this powerful engine of destruction was submitted to its first test. We had gone upon the roof of Mr. Edison's laboratory and the inventor held the little instrument, with its attached mirror, in his hand. We looked about for some object on which to try its powers. On a bare limb of a tree not far away, for it was late in the Fall, sat a disconsolate crow.

"Good," said Mr. Edison, "that will do." He touched a button at the side of the instrument and a soft, whirring noise was heard.

"Feathers," said Mr. Edison, "have a vibration period of three hundred and eighty-six million per second."

He adjusted the index as he spoke. Then, through a sighting tube, he aimed at the bird.

"Now watch," he said.

The Crow's Fate.

Another soft whirr in the instrument, a momentary flash of light close around it, and, behold, the crow had turned from black to white!

"Its feathers are gone," said the inventor; "they have been dissipated into their constituent atoms. Now, we will finish the crow."

The First Test of the Disintegrator.

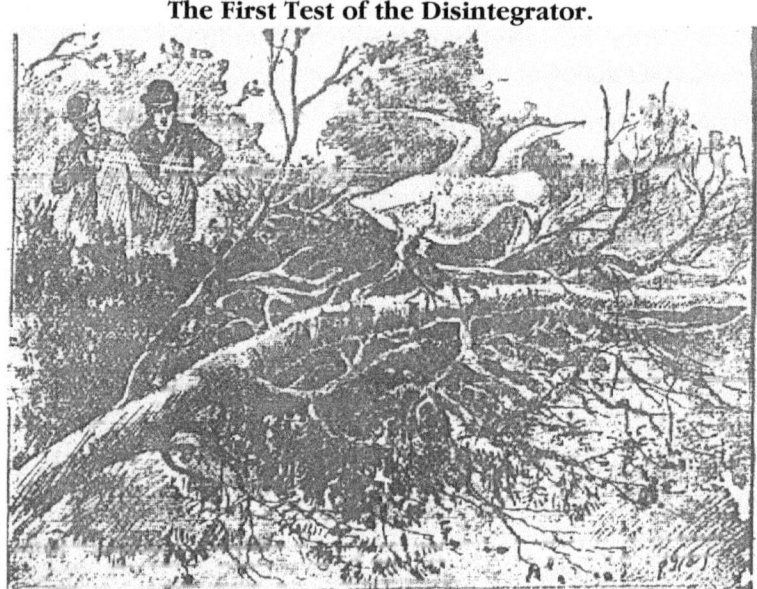

Another soft whirr in the instrument, a momentary flash of light close around it, and, behold, the crow had turned from black to white!

Instantly there was another adjustment of the index, another outshooting of vibratory force, a rapid up and down motion of the index to include a certain range of vibrations, and the crow itself was gone—vanished in empty space! There was the bare twig on which a moment before it had stood. Behind, in the sky, was the white cloud against which its black form had been sharply outlined, but there was no more crow.

Bad for the Martians.

"That looks bad for the Martians, doesn't it?" said the Wizard. "I have ascertained the vibration rate of all the materials of which their war engines whose remains we have collected together are composed. They can be shattered into nothingness in the fraction of a second. Even if the vibration period were not known, it could quickly be hit upon by simply running through the gamut."

"Hurrah!" cried one of the onlookers. "We have met the Martians and they are ours."

Such in brief was the first of the contrivances which Mr. Edison invented for the approaching war with Mars.

And these facts had become widely known. Additional experiments had completed the demonstration of the inventor's ability, with the aid of his wonderful instrument, to destroy any given object, or any part of an object, provided that that part differed in its atomic constitution, and consequently in its vibratory period, from the other parts.

A most impressive public exhibition of the powers of the little disintegrator was given amid the ruins of New York. On lower Broadway a part of the walls of one of the gigantic buildings, which had been destroyed by the Martians, impended in such a manner that it threatened at any moment to fall upon the heads of the passers-by. The Fire Department did not dare touch it. To blow it up seemed a dangerous expedient, because already new buildings had been erected in its neighborhood, and their safety would be imperiled by the flying fragments. The fact happened to come to my knowledge.

"Here is an opportunity," I said to Mr. Edison, "to try the powers of your machine on a large scale."

"Capital!" he instantly replied. "I shall go at once."

Disintegrating a Building.

For the work now in hand it was necessary to employ a battery of disintegrators, since the field of destruction covered by each was comparatively limited. All of the impending portions of the wall must be destroyed at once and together, for otherwise the danger would rather be accentuated than annihilated. The disintegrators were placed upon the roof of a neighboring building, so adjusted that their fields of destruction overlapped one another upon the wall. Their indexes were all set to correspond with the vibration period of the peculiar kind of brick of which the wall consisted. Then the energy was turned on, and a shout of wonder arose from the multitudes which had assembled at a safe distance to witness the experiment.

Only a Cloud Remained.

The wall did not fall; it did not break asunder; no fragments shot this way and that and high in the air; there was no explosion; no shock or noise disturbed the still atmosphere—only a soft whirr, that seemed to pervade everything and to tingle in the nerves of the spectators; and—what had been was not! The wall was gone! But high above and all around the place where it had hung over the street with its threat of death there appeared, swiftly billowing outward in every direction, a faint, bluish cloud. It was the scattered atoms of the destroyed wall.

A Marvellous Scientific Triumph.

Only a soft whirr, that seemed to pervade everything and to tingle in the nerves of the spectators, and—what had been was not! The wall was gone!

And now the cry "On to Mars!" was heard on all sides. But for such an enterprise funds were needed—millions upon millions. Yet some of the fairest and richest portions of the earth had been impoverished by the frightful ravages of those enemies who had dropped down upon them from the skies. Still, the money must be had. The salvation of the planet, as everybody was now convinced, depended upon the successful negotiation of a gigantic war fund, in comparison with which all the expenditures in all of the wars that had been waged by the nations for 2,000 years would be insignificant. The electrical ships and the vibration engines must be constructed by scores and thousands. Only Mr. Edison's immense resources and unrivaled equipment had enabled him to make the models whose powers had been so satisfactorily shown. But to multiply these upon a war scale was not only beyond the resources of any individual—hardly a nation on the globe in the period of its greatest prosperity could have undertaken such a work. All the nations, then, must now conjoin. They must unite their resources, and, if necessary, exhaust all their hoards, in order to raise the needed sum.

The Yankees Lead.

Negotiations were at once begun. The United States naturally took the lead, and their leadership was never for a moment questioned abroad.

Washington was selected as the place of meeting for a great congress of the nations. Washington, luckily, had been one of the places which had not been touched by the Martians. But if Washington had been a city composed of hotels alone, and every hotel so great as to be a little city in itself, it would have been utterly insufficient for the accommodation of the innumerable throngs which now flocked to the banks of the Potomac. But when was American enterprise unequal to a crisis? The necessary hotels, lodging houses and restaurants were constructed with astounding rapidity. One could see the city growing and expanding day by day and week after week. It flowed over Georgetown Heights; it leaped the Potomac; it spread east and west, south and north; square mile after square mile of territory was buried under the advancing buildings, until the gigantic city, which had thus grown up like a mushroom in a night, was fully capable of accommodating all its expected guests.

At first it had been intended that the heads of the various governments should in person attend this universal congress, but as the enterprise went on, as the enthusiasm spread, as the necessity for haste became more apparent through the warning notes which were constantly sounded from the observatories where the astronomers were nightly beholding new evidences of threatening preparations in Mars, the kings and queens of the old world felt that they could not remain at home; that their proper place was at the new focus and centre of the whole world—the city of Washington. Without concerted action, without interchange of suggestion, this impulse seemed to seize all the old world monarchs at once. Suddenly cablegrams flashed to the Government at Washington, announcing that Queen Victoria, the Emperor William, the Czar Nicholas, Alphonso of Spain, with his mother, Maria Christina; the old Emperor Francis Joseph and the Empress Elizabeth, of Austria; King Oscar and Queen Sophia, of Sweden and Norway; King Humbert and Queen Margherita, of Italy; King George and Queen Olga, of Greece; Abdul Hamid, of Turkey; Tsait'ien, Emperor of China; Mutsuhito, the Japanese Mikado, with his beautiful Princess Haruko; the President of France, the President of Switzerland, the First Syndic of the little republic of Andorra, perched on the crest of the Pyrenees, and the heads of all the Central and South American republics, were coming to Washington to take part in the deliberations, which, it was felt, were to settle the fate of earth and Mars.

One day, after this announcement had been received, and the additional news had come that nearly all the visiting monarchs had set out, attended by brilliant suites and convoyed by fleets of warships, for their destination, some coming across the Atlantic to the port of New York, others across the Pacific to San Francisco, Mr. Edison said to me:

"This will be a fine spectacle. Would you like to watch it?"

"Certainly," I replied.

A Grand Spectacle.

The Ship of Space was immediately at our disposal. I think I have not yet mentioned the fact that the inventor's control over the electrical generator carried in the car was so perfect that by varying the potential or changing the polarity he could cause it slowly or swiftly, as might be desired, to approach or recede from any object. The only practical difficulty was presented when the polarity of the electrical charge upon an object in the neighborhood of the car was unknown to those in the car, and happened to be opposite to that of the charge which the car, at that particular moment, was bearing. In such a case, of course, the car would fly toward the object, whatever it might be, like a pith ball or a feather, attracted to the knob of an electrical machine. In this way, considerable danger was occasionally encountered, and a few accidents could not be avoided. Fortunately, however, such cases were rare. It was only now and then that, owing to some local cause, electrical polarities unknown to or unexpected by the navigators, endangered the safety of the car. As I shall have occasion to relate, however, in the course of the narrative, this danger became more acute and assumed at times a most formidable phase, when we had ventured outside the sphere of the earth and were moving through the unexplored regions beyond.

On this occasion, having embarked, we rose rapidly to a height of some thousands of feet and directed our course over the Atlantic. When half way to Ireland, we beheld, in the distance, steaming westward, the smoke of several fleets. As we drew nearer a marvellous spectacle unfolded itself to our eyes. From the northeast, their great guns flashing in the sunlight and their huge funnels belching black volumes that rested like thunder clouds upon the sea, came the mighty warships of England, with her meteor flag streaming red in the breeze, while the royal insignia, indicating the presence of the ruler of the British Empire, was conspicuously displayed upon the flagship of the squadron.

Following a course more directly westward appeared, under another black cloud of smoke, the hulls and guns and burgeons of another great fleet, carrying the tri-color of France, and bearing in its midst the head of the magnificent republic of western Europe.

Further south, beating up against the northerly winds, came a third fleet with the gold and red of Spain fluttering from its masthead. This, too, was carrying its King westward, where now, indeed, the star of empire had taken its way.

Universal Brotherhood.

Rising a little higher, so as to extend our horizon, we saw coming down the English channel, behind the British fleet, the black ships of Russia. Side by side, or following one another's lead, these war fleets were on a peaceful voyage that belied their threatening appearance. There had been no thought of danger to or from the forts and ports of rival nations which they had passed. There was no enmity, and no fear between them when the throats of their ponderous guns yawned at one another across the waves. They were now, in spirit, all one fleet, having one object, bearing against one enemy, ready to defend but one country, and that country was the entire earth.

It was some time before we caught sight of the Emperor William's fleet. It seems that the Kaiser, although at first consenting to the arrangement by which Washington had been selected as the assembling place for the nations, afterwards objected to it.

Kaiser Wilhelm's Jealousy.

"I ought to do this thing myself," he had said. "My glorious ancestors would never have consented to allow these upstart Republicans to lead in a warlike enterprise of this kind. What would my grandfather have said to it? I suspect that it is some scheme aimed at the divine right of kings."

But the good sense of the German people would not suffer their ruler to place them in a position so false and so untenable. And swept along by their enthusiasm the Kaiser had at last consented to embark on his flagship at Kiel, and now he was following the other fleets on their great mission to the Western Continent.

Why did they bring their warships when their intentions were peaceable, do you ask? Well, it was partly the effect of ancient habit, and partly due to the fact that such multitudes of officials and members of ruling families wished to embark for Washington that the ordinary means of ocean communications would have been utterly inadequate to convey them.

After we had feasted our eyes on this strange sight, Mr. Edison suddenly exclaimed: "Now let us see the fellows from the rising sun."

Over the Mississippi.

The car was immediately directed toward the west. We rapidly approached the American coast, and as we sailed over the Alleghany Mountains and the broad plains of the Ohio and the Mississippi, we saw crawling beneath us from west, south and north, an endless succession of railway trains bearing their multitudes on to Washington. With marvellous speed we rushed westward, rising high to skim over the snow-topped peaks of the Rocky Mountains and then the glittering rim of the Pacific was before us. Half way between the American coast and Hawaii we met the fleets coming from China and Japan. Side by side they were ploughing the main, having forgotten, or laid aside, all the animosities of their former wars.

I well remember how my heart was stirred at this impressive exhibition of the boundless influence which my country had come to exercise over all the people of the world, and I turned to look at the man to whose genius this uprising of the earth was due. But Mr. Edison, after his wont, appeared totally unconscious of the fact that he was personally responsible for what was going on. His mind, seemingly, was entirely absorbed in considering problems, the solution of which might be essential to our success in the terrific struggle which was soon to begin.

Back to Washington.

"Well, have you seen enough?" he asked. "Then let us go back to Washington."

As we speeded back across the continent we beheld beneath us again the burdened express trains rushing toward the Atlantic, and hundreds of thousands of upturned eyes watched our swift progress, and volleys of cheers reached our ears, for every one knew that this was Edison's electrical warship, on which the hope of the nation, and the hopes of all the nations, depended. These scenes were repeated again and again until the car hovered over the still expanding capital on the Potomac, where the unceasing ring of hammers rose to the clouds.

Chapter III

The day appointed for the assembling of the nations in Washington opened bright and beautiful. Arrangements had been made for the reception of the distinguished guests at the Capitol. No time was to be wasted, and, having assembled in the Senate Chamber, the business that had called them together was to be immediately begun. The scene in Pennsylvania avenue, when the procession of dignitaries and royalties passed up toward the Capitol, was one never to be forgotten. Bands were playing, magnificent equipages flashed in the morning sunlight, the flags of every nation on the earth fluttered in the breeze. Queen Victoria, with the Prince of Wales escorting her, and riding in an open carriage, was greeted with roars of cheers; the Emperor William, following in another carriage with Empress Victoria at his side, condescended to bow and smile in response to the greetings of a free people. Each of the other monarchs was received in a similar manner. The Czar of Russia proved to be an especial favorite with the multitude on account of the ancient friendship of his house for America. But the greatest applause of all came when the President of France, followed by the President of Switzerland and the First Syndic of the little Republic of Andorra, made their appearance. Equally warm were the greetings extended to the representatives of Mexico and the South American States.

The Sultan of Turkey.

The crowd apparently hardly knew at first how to receive the Sultan of Turkey, but the universal good feeling was in his favor, and finally rounds of hand clapping and cheers greeted his progress along the splendid avenue.

A happy idea had apparently occurred to the Emperor of China and the Mikado of Japan, for, attended by their intermingled suites, they rode together in a single carriage. This object lesson in the unity of international feeling immensely pleased the spectators.

An Unparallelled Scene.

The scene in the Senate Chamber stirred every one profoundly. That it was brilliant and magnificent goes without saying, but there was a seriousness, an intense feeling of expectancy, pervading both those who looked on and those who were to do the work for which these magnates of the earth had assembled, which produced an ineradicable impression. The President of the United States, of course, presided. Representatives of the greater powers occupied the front seats, and some of them were honored with special chairs near the President.

No time was wasted in preliminaries. The President made a brief speech.

"We have come together," he said, "to consider a question that equally interests the whole earth. I need not remind you that unexpectedly and without provocation on our part the people—the monsters, I should rather say—of Mars, recently came down upon the earth, attacked us in our homes and spread desolation around them. Having the advantage of ages of evolution, which for us are yet in the future, they brought with them engines of death and of destruction against which we found it impossible to contend. It is within the memory of every one in reach of my voice that it was through the entirely unexpected succor which Providence sent us that we were suddenly and effectually freed from the invaders. By our own efforts we could have done nothing."

McKinley's Tribute.

"But, as you all know, the first feeling of relief which followed the death of our foes was quickly succeeded by the fearful news which came to us from the observatories, that the Martians were undoubtedly preparing for a second invasion of our planet. Against this we should have had no recourse and no hope but for the genius of one of my countrymen, who, as you are all aware, has perfected means which may enable us not only to withstand the attack of those awful enemies, but to meet them, and, let us hope, to conquer them on their own ground."

"Mr. Edison is here to explain to you what those means are. But we have also another object. Whether we send a fleet of interplanetary ships to invade Mars or whether we simply confine our attention to works of defence, in either case it will be necessary to raise a very large sum of money. None of us has yet recovered from the effects of the recent invasion. The earth is poor to-day compared to its position a few years ago; yet we cannot allow our poverty to stand in the way. The money, the means, must be had. It will be part of our business here to raise a gigantic war fund by the aid of which we can construct the equipment and machinery that we shall require. This, I think, is all I need to say. Let us proceed to business."

"Where is Mr. Edison?" cried a voice.

"Will Mr. Edison please step forward?" said the President.

There was a stir in the assembly, and the iron-gray head of the great inventor was seen moving through the crowd. In his hand he carried one of his marvellous disintegrators. He was requested to explain and illustrate its operation. Mr. Edison smiled.

Edison to the Rescue of the Universe.

"Will Mr. Edison please step forward?" said the President. There was a stir in the assembly, and the iron gray head of the great inventor was seen moving through the crowd. In his hand he carried one of his marvellous disintegrators.

Edison to the Rescue.

"I can explain its details," he said, "to Lord Kelvin, for instance, but if Their Majesties will excuse me, I doubt whether I can make it plain to the crowned heads."

The Emperor William smiled superciliously. Apparently he thought that another assault had been committed upon the divine right of kings. But the Czar Nicholas appeared to be amused, and the Emperor of China, who had been studying English, laughed in his sleeve, as if he suspected that a joke had been perpetrated.

"I think," said one of the deputies, "that a simple exhibition of the powers of the instrument, without a technical explanation of its method of working, will suffice for our purpose."

This suggestion was immediately approved. In response to it, Mr. Edison, by a few simple experiments, showed how he could quickly and certainly shatter into its constituent atoms any object upon which the vibratory force of the disintegrator should be directed. In this manner he caused an inkstand to disappear under the very nose of the Emperor William without a spot of ink being scattered upon his sacred person, but evidently the odor of the disunited atoms was not agreeable to the nostrils of the Kaiser.

Mr. Edison also explained in general terms the principle on which the instrument worked. He was greeted with round after round of applause, and the spirit of the assembly rose high.

Next the workings of the electrical ship were explained, and it was announced that after the meeting had adjourned an exhibition of the flying powers of the ship would be given in the open air.

These experiments, together with the accompanying explanations, added to what had already been disseminated through the public press, were quite sufficient to convince all the representatives who had assembled in Washington that the problem of how to conquer the Martians had been solved. The means were plainly at hand. It only remained to apply them. For this purpose, as the President had pointed out, it would be necessary to raise a very large sum of money.

"How much will be needed?" asked one of the English representatives.

"At least ten thousand millions of dollars," replied the President.

"It would be safer," said a Senator from the Pacific Coast, "to make it twenty-five thousand millions."

"I suggest," said the King of Italy, "that the nations be called in alphabetical order, and that the representatives of each name a sum which it is ready and able to contribute."

"We want the cash or its equivalent," shouted the Pacific Coast Senator.

"I shall not follow the alphabet strictly," said the President, "but shall begin with the larger nations first. Perhaps, under the circumstances, it is proper that the United States should lead the way. Mr. Secretary," he continued, turning to the Secretary of the Treasury, "how much can we stand?"

An Enormous Sum.

"At least a thousand millions," replied the Secretary of the Treasury.

A roar of applause that shook the room burst from the assembly. Even some of the monarchs threw up their hats. The Emperor Tsait'ten smiled from ear to ear. One of the Roko Tuis, or native chiefs, from Fiji, sprang up and brandished a war club.

Enthusiasm in the Assembly.

One of the Roko Tuis, or native chiefs from Fiji, sprang up and brandished a war club.

The President then proceeded to call the other nations, beginning with Austria-Hungary and ending with Zanzibar, whose Sultan, Hamoud bin Mahomed, had come to the congress in the escort of Queen Victoria. Each contributed liberally.

Germany coming in alphabetical order just before Great Britain, had named, through its Chancellor, the sum of

$500,000,000, but when the First Lord of the British Treasury, not wishing to be behind the United States, named double that sum as the contribution of the British Empire, the Emperor William looked displeased. He spoke a word in the ear of the Chancellor, who immediately raised his hand.

A Thousand Million Dollars.

"We will give a thousand million dollars," said the Chancellor.

Queen Victoria seemed surprised, though not displeased. The First Lord of the Treasury met her eye, and then, rising in his place, said:

"Make it fifteen hundred million for Great Britain."

Emperor William consulted again with his Chancellor, but evidently concluded not to increase his bid.

But, at any rate, the fund had benefited to the amount of a thousand millions by this little outburst of imperial rivalry.

The greatest surprise of all, however, came when the King of Siam was called upon for his contribution. He had not been given a foremost place in the Congress, but when the name of his country was pronounced he rose by his chair, dressed in a gorgeous specimen of the peculiar attire of his country, then slowly pushed his way to the front, stepped up to the President's desk and deposited upon it a small box.

"This is our contribution," he said, in broken English.

The cover was lifted, and there darted, shimmering in the half gloom of the Chamber, a burst of iridescence from the box.

The Long Lost Treasure.

"My friends of the Western world," continued the King of Siam, "will be interested in seeing this gem. Only once before has the eye of a European been blessed with the sight of it. Your books will tell you that in the seventeenth century a traveler, Tavernier, saw in India an unmatched diamond which afterward disappeared like a meteor, and was thought to have been lost from the earth. You all know the name of that diamond and its history. It is the Great Mogul, and it lies before you. How it came into my possession I shall not explain. At any rate, it is honestly mine, and I freely contribute it here to aid in protecting my native planet against those enemies who appear determined to destroy it."

The King of Siam's Contribution.

"This is our contribution," he said, in broken English. The cover was lifted, there darted, shimmering in the half gloom of the chamber, a burst of iridescence from the box.

When the excitement which the appearance of this long lost treasure, that had been the subject of so many romances and of such long and fruitless search, had subsided, the President continued calling the list, until he had completed it.

Upon taking the sum of the contributions (the Great Mogul was reckoned at three millions) it was found to be still one thousand millions short of the required amount.

The Secretary of the Treasury was instantly on his feet.

"Mr. President," he said, "I think we can stand that addition. Let it be added to the contribution of the United States of America."

When the cheers that greeted the conclusion of the business were over, the President announced that the next affair of the Congress was to select a director who should have entire charge of the preparations for the war. It was the universal sentiment that no man could be so well suited for this post as Mr. Edison himself. He was accordingly selected by the unanimous and enthusiastic choice of the great assembly.

"How long a time do you require to put everything in readiness?" asked the President.

"Give me carte blanche," replied Mr. Edison, "and I believe I can have a hundred electric ships and three thousand disintegrators ready within six months."

A tremendous cheer greeted this announcement.

"Your powers are unlimited," said the President, "draw on the fund for as much money as you need," whereupon the Treasurer of the United States was made the disbursing officer of the fund, and the meeting adjourned.

Not less than 5,000,000 people had assembled at Washington from all parts of the world. Every one of this immense multitude had been able to listen to the speeches and the cheers in the Senate chamber, although not personally present there. Wires had been run all over the city, and hundreds of improved telephonic receivers provided, so that every one could hear. Even those who were unable to visit Washington, people living in Baltimore, New York, Boston, and as far away as New Orleans, St. Louis and Chicago, had also listened to the proceedings with the aid of these receivers. Upon the whole, probably not less than 50,000,000 people had heard the deliberations of the great congress of the nations.

The Excitement in Washington.

The telegraph and the cable had sent the news across the oceans to all the capitols of the earth. The exultation was so great that the people seemed mad with joy.

The promised exhibition of the electrical ship took place the next day. Enormous multitudes witnessed the experiment, and there was a struggle for places in the car. Even Queen Victoria, accompanied by the Prince of Wales, ventured to take a ride in it, and they enjoyed it so much that Mr. Edison prolonged the journey as far as Boston and the Bunker Hill monument.

Most of the other monarchs also took a high ride, but when the turn of the Emperor of China came he repeated a fable which he said had come down from the time of Confucius:

A Chinese Legend.

"Once upon a time there was a Chinaman living in the valley of the Hoang-Ho River, who was accustomed frequently to lie on his back, gazing at, and envying, the birds that he saw flying away in the sky. One day he saw a black speck which rapidly grew larger and larger, until as it got near he perceived that it was an enormous bird, which overshadowed the earth with its wings. It was the elephant of birds, the roc. 'Come with me,' said the roc, 'and I will show you the wonders of the kingdom of the birds.' The man caught hold of its claw and nestled among its feathers, and they rapidly rose high in the air, and sailed away to the Kuen-Lun Mountains. Here, as they passed near the top of the peaks, another roc made its appearance. The wings of the two great birds brushed together, and immediately they fell to fighting. In the midst of the melee the man lost his hold and tumbled into the top of a tree, where his pigtail caught on a branch, and he remained suspended. There the unfortunate man hung helpless, until a rat, which had its home in the rocks at the foot of the tree, took compassion upon him, and, climbing up, gnawed off the branch. As the man slowly and painfully wended his weary way homeward, he said: 'This teaches me that creatures to whom nature has given neither feathers nor wings should leave the kingdom of the birds to those who are fitted to inhabit it.'"

Having told this story, Tsait'ien turned his back on the electrical ship.

The Grand Ball.

After the exhibition was finished, and amid the fresh outburst of enthusiasm that followed, it was suggested that a proper way to wind up the Congress and give suitable expression to the festive mood which now possessed mankind would be to have a grand ball. This suggestion met with immediate and universal approval.

But for so gigantic an affair it was, of course, necessary to make special preparations. A convenient place was selected on the Virginia side of the Potomac; a space of ten acres was carefully levelled and covered with a polished floor, rows of columns one hundred feet apart were run across it in every direction, and these were decorated with electric lights, displaying every color of the spectrum.

Unsurpassed Fireworks.

Above this immense space, rising in the centre to a height of more than a thousand feet, was anchored a vast number of balloons, all aglow with lights, and forming a tremendous dome, in which brilliant lamps were arranged in such a manner as to exhibit, in an endless succession of combinations, all the national colors, ensigns and insignia of the various countries represented at the Congress. Blazing eagles, lions, unicorns, dragons and other imaginary creatures that the different nations had chosen for their symbols appeared to hover high above the dancers, shedding a brilliant light upon the scene.

Circles of magnificent thrones were placed upon the floor in convenient locations for seeing. A thousand bands of music played, and tens of thousands of couples, gayly dressed and flashing with gems, whirled together upon the polished floor.

Queen Victoria Dances.

The Queen of England led the dance, on the arm of the President of the United States.

The Prince of Wales led forth the fair daughter of the President, universally admired as the most beautiful woman upon the great ballroom floor.

The Emperor William, in his military dress, danced with the beauteous Princess Masaco, the daughter of the Mikado, who wore for the occasion the ancient costume of the women of her country, sparkling with jewels, and glowing with quaint combinations of color like a gorgeous butterfly.

The Chinese Emperor, with his pigtail flying high as he spun, danced with the Empress of Russia.

The King of Siam essayed a waltz with the Queen Ranavalona, of Madagascar, while the Sultan of Turkey basked in the smiles of a Chicago heiress to a hundred millions.

The Czar choose for his partner a dark-eyed beauty from Peru, but King Malietoa, of Samoa, was suspicious of civilized charmers and, avoiding all of their allurements, expressed his joy and gave vent to his enthusiasm in a pas seul. In this he was quickly joined by a band of Sioux Indian chiefs, whose whoops and yells so startled the leader of a German band on their part of the floor that he dropped his baton and, followed by the musicians, took to his heels.

This incident amused the good-natured Emperor of China more than anything else that had occurred.

"Make muchee noisee," he said, indicating the fleeing musicians with his thumb. "Allee same muchee flaid noisee," and then his round face dimpled into another laugh.

The scene from the outside was even more imposing than that which greeted the eye within the brilliantly lighted enclosure. Far away in the night, rising high among the stars, the vast dome of illuminated balloons seemed like some supernatural creation, too grand and glorious to have been constructed by the inhabitants of the earth.

All around it, and from some of the balloons themselves, rose jets and fountains of fire, ceaselessly playing, and blotting out the constellations of the heavens by their splendor.

The Prince of Wales's Toast.

The dance was followed by a grand banquet, at which the Prince of Wales proposed a toast to Mr. Edison:

"It gives me much pleasure," he said, "to offer, in the name of the nations of the Old World, this tribute of our admiration for, and our confidence in, the genius of the New World. Perhaps on such an occasion as this, when all racial differences and prejudices ought to be, and are, buried and forgotten, I should not recall anything that might revive them; yet I cannot refrain from expressing my happiness in knowing that the champion who is to achieve the salvation of the earth has come forth from the bosom of the Anglo-Saxon race."

Several of the great potentates looked grave upon hearing the Prince of Wales's words, and the Czar and the Kaiser exchanged glances; but there was no interruption to the cheers that followed. Mr. Edison, whose modesty and dislike to display and to speechmaking were well known, simply said:

"I think we have got the machine that can whip them. But we ought not to be wasting any time. Probably they are not dancing on Mars, but are getting ready to make us dance."

Haste to Embark.

These words instantly turned the current of feeling in the vast assembly. There was no longer any disposition to expend time in vain boastings and rejoicings. Everywhere the cry now became, "Let us make haste! Let us get ready at once! Who knows but the Martians have already embarked, and are now on their way to destroy us?"

Under the impulse of this new feeling, which, it must be admitted, was very largely inspired by terror, the vast ballroom was quickly deserted. The lights were suddenly put out in the great dome of balloons, for someone had whispered:

"Suppose they should see that from Mars? Would they not guess what we were about, and redouble their preparations to finish us?"

Upon the suggestion of the President of the United States, an executive committee, representing all the principal nations, was appointed, and without delay a meeting of this committee was assembled at the White House. Mr. Edison was summoned before it, and asked to sketch briefly the plan upon which he proposed to work.

Thousands of Men for Mars.

I need not enter into the details of what was done at this meeting. Let it suffice to say that when it broke up, in the small hours of the morning, it had been unanimously resolved that as many thousands of men as Mr. Edison might require should be immediately placed at his disposal; that as far as possible all the great manufacturing establishments of the country should be instantly transformed into factories where electrical ships and disintegrators could be built, and upon the suggestion of Professor Sylvanus P. Thompson, the celebrated English electrical expert, seconded by Lord Kelvin, it was resolved that all the leading men of science in the world should place their services at the disposal of Mr. Edison in any capacity in which, in his judgment, they might be useful to him.

The members of this committee were disposed to congratulate one another on the good work which they had so promptly accomplished, when at the moment of their adjournment, a telegraphic dispatch was handed to the President from Professor George E. Hale, the director of the great Yerkes Observatory, in Wisconsin. The telegram read:

What's Happening on Mars?

"Professor Barnard, watching Mars to-night with the forty-inch telescope, saw a sudden outburst of reddish light, which we think indicates that something has been shot from the planet. Spectroscopic observations of this moving light indicated that it was coming earthward, while visible, at the rate of not less than one hundred miles a second."

Hardly had the excitement caused by the reading of this dispatch subsided, when others of a similar import came from the Lick Observatory, in California; from the branch of the Harvard Observatory at Arequipa, in Peru, and from the Royal Observatory, at Potsdam.

When the telegram from this last-named place was read the Emperor William turned to his Chancellor and said:

"I want to go home. If I am to die I prefer to leave my bones among those of my Imperial ancestors, and not in this vulgar country, where no king has ever ruled. I don't like this atmosphere. It makes me feel limp."

And now, whipped on by the lash of alternate hope and fear, the earth sprang to its work of preparation.

Chapter IV

It is not necessary for me to describe the manner in which Mr. Edison performed his tremendous task. He was as good as his word, and within six months from the first stroke of the hammer, a hundred electrical ships, each provided with a full battery of disintegrators, were floating in the air above the harbor and the partially rebuilt city of New York.

It was a wonderful scene. The polished sides of the huge floating cars sparkled in the sunlight, and, as they slowly rose and fell, and swung this way and that, upon the tides of the air, as if held by invisible cables, the brilliant pennons streaming from their peaks waved up and down like the wings of an assemblage of gigantic humming birds.

The Departure of the Flying Ships on Their Marvellous Errand to Mars.

It was a wonderful scene. The polished sides of the huge floating cars sparkled in the sunlight, and, as they slowly rose and fell, and swung this way and that, upon the tides of the air, as if held by invisible cables, the brilliant pennons streaming from their peaks waved up and down like the the wings of an assemblage of gigantic humming birds.

Not knowing whether the atmosphere of Mars would prove suitable to be breathed by inhabitants of the earth, Mr. Edison had made provision, by means of an abundance of glass-protected openings, to permit the inmates of the electrical ships to survey their surroundings without quitting the interior. It was possible by properly selecting the rate of undulation, to pass the vibratory impulse from the disintegrators through the glass windows of a car, without damage to the glass itself. The windows were so arranged that the disintegrators could sweep around the car on all sides, and could also be directed above or below, as necessity might dictate.

To overcome the destructive forces employed by the Martians no satisfactory plan had yet been devised, because there was no means to experiment with them. The production of those forces was still the secret of our enemies. But Mr. Edison had no doubt that if we could not resist their effects we might at least be able to avoid them by the rapidity of our motions. As he pointed out, the war machines which the Martians had employed in their invasion of the earth, were really very awkward and unmanageable affairs. Mr. Edison's electrical ships, on the other hand, were marvels of speed and of manageability. They could dart about, turn, reverse their course, rise, fall, with the quickness and ease of a fish in the water. Mr. Edison calculated that even if mysterious bolts should fall upon our ships we could diminish their power to cause injury by our rapid evolutions.

We might be deceived in our expectations, and might have overestimated our powers, but at any rate we must take our chances and try.

Watching the Martians.

A multitude, exceeding even that which had assembled during the great congress at Washington, now thronged New York and its neighborhood to witness the mustering and the departure of the ships bound for Mars. Nothing further had been heard of the mysterious phenomenon reported from the observatories six months before, and which at the time was believed to indicate the departure of another expedition from Mars for the invasion of the earth. If the Martians had set out to attack us they had evidently gone astray; or, perhaps, it was some other world that they were aiming at this time.

The expedition had, of course, profoundly stirred the interest of the scientific world, and representatives of every branch of science, from all the civilized nations, urged their claims to places in the ships. Mr. Edison was compelled, from lack of room, to refuse transportation to more than one in a thousand of those who now, on the plea that they might be able to bring back something of advantage to science, wished to embark for Mars.

As the Great Napoleon Did.

On the model of the celebrated corps of literary and scientific men which Napoleon carried with him in his invasion of Egypt, Mr. Edison selected a company of the foremost astronomers, archaeologists, anthropologists, botanists, bacteriologists, chemists, physicists, mathematicians, mechanicians, meteorologists and experts in mining, metallurgy and every other branch of practical science, as well as artists and photographers. It was but reasonable to believe that in another world, and a world so much older than the earth as Mars was, these men would be able to gather materials in comparison with which the discoveries made among the ruins of ancient empires in Egypt and Babylonia would be insignificant indeed.

To Conquer Another World.

It was a wonderful undertaking and a strange spectacle. There was a feeling of uncertainty which awed the vast multitude whose eyes were upturned to the ships. The expedition was not large, considering the gigantic character of the undertaking. Each of the electrical ships carried about twenty men, together with an abundant supply of compressed provisions, compressed air, scientific apparatus and so on. In all, there were about 2,000 men, who were going to conquer, if they could, another world!

But though few in numbers, they represented the flower of the earth, the culmination of the genius of the planet. The greatest leaders in science, both theoretical and practical, were there. It was the evolution of the earth against the evolution of Mars. It was a planet in the heyday of its strength matched against an aged and decrepit world which, nevertheless, in consequence of its long ages of existence, had acquired an experience which made it a most dangerous foe. On both sides there was desperation. The earth was desperate because it foresaw destruction unless it could first destroy its enemy. Mars was desperate because nature was gradually depriving it of the means of supporting life, and its teeming population was compelled to swarm like the inmates of an overcrowded hive of bees, and find new homes elsewhere. In this respect the situation on Mars, as we were well aware, resembled what had already been known upon the earth, where the older nations overflowing with population had sought new lands in which to settle, and for that purpose had driven out the native inhabitants, whenever those natives had proven unable to resist the invasion.

No man could foresee the issue of what we were about to undertake, but the tremendous powers which the disintegrators had exhibited and the marvellous efficiency of the electrical ships bred almost universal confidence that we should be successful.

Master Minds of the World.

The car in which Mr. Edison travelled was, of course, the flagship of the squadron, and I had the good fortune to be included among its inmates. Here, besides several leading men of science from our own country, were Lord Kelvin, Lord Rayleigh, Professor Roentgen, Dr. Moissan—the man who first made artificial diamonds—and several others whose fame had encircled the world. Each of these men cherished hopes of wonderful discoveries, along his line of investigation, to be made in Mars.

An elaborate system of signals had, of course, to be devised for the control of the squadron. These signals consisted of brilliant electric lights displayed at night and so controlled that by their means long sentences and directions could be easily and quickly transmitted.

A Novel Signal System.

The day signals consisted partly of brightly colored pennons and flags, which were to serve only when, shadowed by clouds or other obstructions, the full sunlight should not fall upon the ships. This could naturally only occur near the surface of the earth or of another planet.

Once out of the shadow of the earth we should have no more clouds and no more night until we arrived at Mars. In open space the sun would be continually shining. It would be perpetual day for us, except as, by artificial means, we furnished ourselves with darkness for the purpose of promoting sleep. In this region of perpetual day, then, the signals were also to be transmitted by flashes of light from mirrors reflecting the rays of the sun.

Perpetual Night!

Yet this perpetual day would be also, in one sense, a perpetual night. There would be no more blue sky for us, because without an atmosphere the sunlight could not be diffused. Objects would be illuminated only on the side toward the sun. Anything that screened off the direct rays of sunlight would produce absolute darkness behind it. There would be no graduation of shadow. The sky would be as black as ink on all sides.

While it was the intention to remain as much as possible within the cars, yet since it was probable that necessity would arise for occasionally quitting the interior of the electrical ships, Mr. Edison had provided for this emergency by inventing an airtight dress constructed somewhat after the manner of a diver's suit, but of much lighter material. Each ship was provided with several of these suits, by wearing which one could venture outside the car even when it was beyond the atmosphere of the earth.

The Air-Tight Suit.

The device employed by the earth's warriors when they reached a point beyond the atmosphere of this planet.

Terrific Cold Anticipated.

Provision had been made to meet the terrific cold which we knew would be encountered the moment we had passed beyond the atmosphere—that awful absolute zero which men had measured by anticipation, but never yet experienced—by a simple system of producing within the air-tight suits a temperature sufficiently elevated to counteract the effects of the frigidity without. By means of long, flexible tubes, air could be continually supplied to the wearers of the suits, and by an ingenious contrivance a store of compressed air sufficient to last for several hours was provided for each suit, so that in case of necessity the wearer could throw off the tubes connecting him with the air tanks in the car. Another object which had been kept in view in the preparation of these suits was the possible exploration of an airless planet, such as the moon.

The necessity of some contrivance by means of which we should be enabled to converse with one another when on the outside of the cars in open space, or when in an airless world, like the moon, where there would be no medium by which the waves of sound could be conveyed as they are in the atmosphere of the earth, had been foreseen by our great inventor, and he had not found it difficult to contrive suitable devices for meeting the emergency.

Inside the headpiece of each of the electrical suits was the mouthpiece of a telephone. This was connected with a wire which, when not in use, could be conveniently coiled upon the arm of the wearer. Near the ears, similarly connected with wires, were telephonic receivers.

An Aerial Telegraph.

When two persons wearing the air-tight dresses wished to converse with one another it was only necessary for them to connect themselves by the wires, and conversation could then be easily carried on.

Careful calculations of the precise distance of Mars from the earth at the time when the expedition was to start had been made by a large number of experts in mathematical astronomy. But it was not Mr. Edison's intention to go direct to Mars. With the exception of the first electrical ship, which he had completed, none had yet been tried in a long voyage. It was desirable that the qualities of each of the ships should first be carefully tested, and for this reason the leader of the expedition determined that the moon should be the first port of space at which the squadron would call.

It chanced that the moon was so situated at this time as to be nearly in a line between the earth and Mars, which latter was in opposition to the sun, and consequently as favorably situated as possible for the purposes of the voyage. What would be, then, for 99 out of the 100 ships of the squadron, a trial trip would at the same time be a step of a quarter of a million of miles gained in the direction of our journey, and so no time would be wasted.

The departure from the earth was arranged to occur precisely at midnight. The moon near the full was hanging high over head, and a marvellous spectacle was presented to the eyes of those below as the great squadron of floating ships, with their signal lights ablaze, cast loose and began slowly to move away on their adventurous and unprecedented expedition into the great unknown. A tremendous cheer, billowing up from the throats of millions of excited men and women, seemed to rend the curtain of the night, and made the airships tremble with the atmospheric vibrations that were set in motion.

Magnificent Fireworks.

Instantly magnificent fireworks were displayed in honor of our departure. Rockets by hundreds of thousands shot heavenward, and then burst in constellations of fiery drops. The sudden illumination thus produced, overspreading hundreds of square miles of the surface of the earth with a light almost like that of day, must certainly have been visible to the inhabitants of Mars, if they were watching us at the time. They might, or might not, correctly interpret its significance; but, at any rate, we did not care. We were off, and were confident that we could meet our enemy on his own ground before he could attack us again.

And the Earth Was Like a Globe.

And now, as we slowly rose higher, a marvellous scene was disclosed. At first the earth beneath us, buried as it was in night, resembled the hollow of a vast cup of ebony blackness, in the centre of which, like the molten lava run together at the bottom of a volcanic crater, shone the light of the illuminations around New York. But when we got beyond the atmosphere, and the earth still continued to recede below us, its aspect changed. The cup-shaped appearance was gone, and it began to round out beneath our eyes in the form of a vast globe—an enormous ball mysteriously suspended under us, glimmering over most of its surface, with the faint illumination of the moon, and showing toward its eastern edge the oncoming light of the rising sun.

When we were still further away, having slightly varied our course so that the sun was once more entirely hidden behind the centre of the earth, we saw its atmosphere completely illuminated, all around it, with prismatic lights, like a gigantic rainbow in the form of a ring.

Another shift in our course rapidly carried us out of the shadow of the earth and into the all pervading sunshine. Then the great planet beneath us hung unspeakable in its beauty. The outlines of several of the continents were clearly discernible on its surface, streaked and spotted with delicate shades of varying color, and the sunlight flashed and glowed in long lanes across the convex surface of the oceans. Parallel with the Equator and along the regions of the ever blowing trade winds, were vast belts of clouds, gorgeous with crimson and purple as the sunlight fell upon them. Immense expanses of snow and ice lay like a glittering garment upon both land and sea around the North Pole.

Farewell To This Terrestrial Sphere.

As we gazed upon this magnificent spectacle, our hearts bounded within us. This was our earth—this was the planet we were going to defend—our home in the trackless wilderness of space. And it seemed to us indeed a home for which we might gladly expend our last breath. A new determination to conquer or die sprung up in our hearts, and I saw Lord Kelvin, after gazing at the beauteous scene which the earth presented through his eyeglass, turn about and peer in the direction in which we knew that Mars lay, with a sudden frown that caused the glass to lose its grip and fall dangling from its string upon his breast. Even Mr. Edison seemed moved.

"I am glad I thought of the disintegrator," he said. "I shouldn't like to see that world down there laid waste again."

"And it won't be," said Professor Sylvanus P. Thompson, gripping the handle of an electric machine, "not if we can help it."

Chapter V

To prevent accidents, it had been arranged that the ships should keep a considerable distance apart. Some of them gradually drifted away, until, on account of the neutral tint of their sides, they were swallowed up in the abyss of space. Still it was possible to know where every member of the squadron was through the constant interchange of signals. These, as I have explained, were effected by means of mirrors flashing back the light of the sun.

But, although it was now unceasing day for us, yet, there being no atmosphere to diffuse the sun's light, the stars were visible to us just as at night upon the earth, and they shone with extraordinary splendor against the intense black background of the firmament. The lights of some of the more distant ships of our squadron were not brighter than the stars in whose neighborhood they seemed to be. In some cases it was only possible to distinguish between the light of a ship and that of a star by the fact that the former was continually flashing while the star was steady in its radiance.

An Uncanny Effect.

The most uncanny effect was produced by the absence of atmosphere around us. Inside the car, where there was air, the sunlight, streaming through one or more of the windows, was diffused and produced ordinary daylight.

But when we ventured outside we could only see things by halves. The side of the car that the sun's rays touched was visible, the other side was invisible, the light from the stars not making it bright enough to affect the eye in contrast with the sun-illuminated half.

As I held up my arm before my eyes, half of it seemed to be shaved off lengthwise; a companion on the deck of the ship looked like half a man. So the other electrical ships near us appeared as half ships, only the illuminated sides being visible.

A Strange Light.

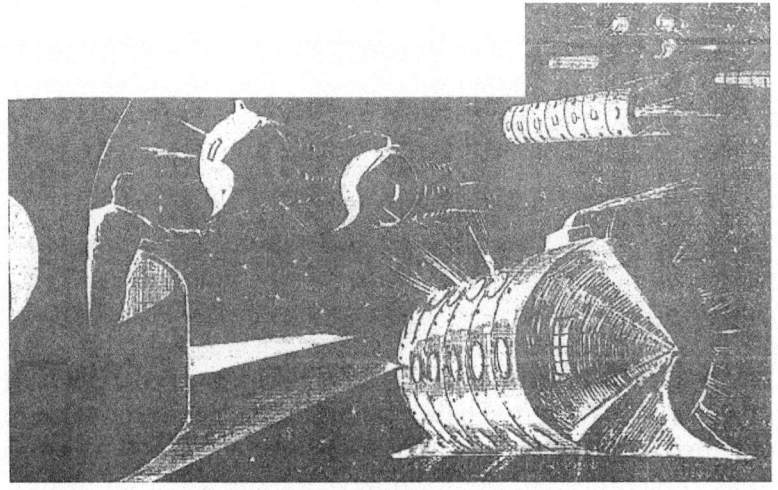

The other electrical ships appeared as half ships, only the illuminated sides being visible.

We had now got so far away that the earth had taken on the appearance of a heavenly body like the moon. Its colors had become all blended into a golden-reddish hue, which overspread nearly its entire surface, except at the poles, where there were broad patches of white. It was marvellous to look at this huge orb behind us, while far beyond it shone the blazing sun like an enormous star in the blackest of nights. In the opposite direction appeared the silver orb of the moon, and scattered all around were millions of brilliant stars, amid which, like fireflies, flashed and sparkled the signal lights of the squadron.

Danger Manifests Itself.

A danger that might easily have been anticipated, that perhaps had been anticipated, but against which it would have been difficult, if not impossible, to provide, presently manifested itself.

Looking out of a window toward the right, I suddenly noticed the lights of a distant ship darting about in a curious curve. Instantly afterward another member of the squadron, nearer by, behaved in the same inexplicable manner. Then two or three of the floating cars seemed to be violently drawn from their courses and hurried rapidly in the direction of the flagship. Immediately I perceived a small object, luridly flaming, which seemed to move with immense speed in our direction.

The truth instantly flashed upon my mind, and I shouted to the other occupants of the car:

Struck By A Meteor!

"A meteor!"

And such indeed it was. We had met this mysterious wanderer in space at a moment when we were moving in a direction at right angles to the path it was pursuing around the sun. Small as it was, and its diameter probably did not exceed a single foot, it was yet an independent little world, and as such a member of the solar system. Its distance from the sun being so near that of the earth, I knew that its velocity, assuming it to be travelling in a nearly circular orbit, must be about eighteen miles in a second. With this velocity, then, it plunged like a projectile shot by some mysterious enemy in space directly through our squadron. It had come and was gone before one could utter a sentence of three words. Its appearance, and the effect it had produced upon the ships in whose neighborhood it passed, indicated that it bore an intense and tremendous charge of electricity. How it had become thus charged I cannot pretend to say. I simply record the fact. And this charge, it was evident, was opposite in polarity to that which the ships of the squadron bore. It therefore exerted an attractive influence upon them and thus drew them after it.

I had just time to think how lucky it was that the meteor did not strike any of us, when, glancing at a ship just ahead, I perceived that an accident had occurred. The ship swayed violently from its course, dazzling flashes played around it, and two or three of the men forming its crew appeared for an instant on its exterior, wildly gesticulating, but almost instantly falling prone.

It was evident at a glance that the car had been struck by the meteor. How serious the damage might be we could not instantly determine. The course of our ship was immediately altered, the electric polarity was changed, and we rapidly approached the disabled car.

The men who had fallen lay upon its surface. One of the heavy circular glasses covering a window had been smashed to atoms.

Through this the meteor had passed, killing two or three men who stood in its course. Then it had crashed through the opposite side of the car, and, passing on, disappeared into space. The store of air contained in the car had immediately rushed out through the openings, and when two or three of us, having donned our air-tight suits as quickly as possible, entered the wrecked car we found all its inmates stretched upon the floor in a condition of asphyxiation. They, as well as those who lay upon the exterior, were immediately removed to the flagship, restoratives were applied, and, fortunately, our aid had come so promptly that the lives of all of them were saved. But life had fled from the mangled bodies of those who had stood directly in the path of the fearful projectile.

A Frightful Tragedy in Space.

Through this the meteor had passed, killing two or three men who stood in its course.

This strange accident had been witnessed by several of the members of the fleet, and they quickly drew together, in order to inquire for the particulars. As the flagship was now overcrowded by the addition of so many men to its crew, Mr. Edison had them distributed among the other cars. Fortunately it happened that the disintegrators contained in the wrecked car were not injured. Mr. Edison thought that it would be possible to repair the car itself, and for that purpose he had it attached to the flagship in order that it might be carried on as far as the moon. The bodies of the dead were transported with it, as it was determined, instead of committing them to the fearful deep of space, where they would have wandered forever, or else have fallen like meteors upon the earth, to give them interment in the lunar soil.

Nearing the Moon.

As we now rapidly approached the moon the change which the appearance of its surface underwent was no less wonderful than that which the surface of the earth had presented in the reverse order while we were receding from it. From a pale silver orb, shining with comparative faintness among the stars, it slowly assumed the appearance of a vast mountainous desert. As we drew nearer its colors became more pronounced; the great flat regions appeared darker; the mountain peaks shone more brilliantly. The huge chasms seemed bottomless and blacker than midnight. Gradually separate mountains appeared. What seemed like expanses of snow and immense glaciers streaming down their sides sparkled with great brilliancy in the perpendicular rays of the sun. Our motion had now assumed the aspect of falling. We seemed to be dropping from an immeasurable height and with an inconceivable velocity, straight down upon those giant peaks.

The Mountains of Luna.

Here and there curious lights glowed upon the mysterious surface of the moon. Where the edge of the moon cut the sky behind it, it was broken and jagged with mountain masses. Vast crater rings overspread its surface, and in some of these I imagined I could perceive a lurid illumination coming out of their deepest cavities, and the curling of mephitic vapors around their terrible jaws.

We were approaching that part of the moon which is known to astronomers as the Bay of Rainbows. Here a huge semi-circular region, as smooth almost as the surface of a prairie, lay beneath our eyes, stretching southward into a vast ocean-like expanse, while on the north it was enclosed by an enormous range of mountain cliffs, rising perpendicularly to a height of many thousands of feet, and rent and gashed in every direction by forces which seemed at some remote period to have labored at tearing this little world in pieces.

A Dead And Mangled World.

The Moon's Strange and Ghastly Surface in Full View of Man.

It was a fearful spectacle; a dead and mangled world, too dreadful to look upon. The idea of the death of the moon was, of course, not a new one to many of us. We had long been aware that the earth's satellite was a body which had passed beyond the stage of life, if indeed it had ever been a life supporting globe; but none of us were prepared for the terrible spectacle which now smote our eyes.

At each end of the semi-circular ridge that encloses the Bay of Rainbows there is a lofty promontory. That at the north-western extremity had long been known to astronomers under the name of Cape Laplace. The other promontory, at the southeastern termination, is called Cape Heraclides. It was toward the latter that we were approaching, and by interchange of signals all the members of the squadron had been informed that Cape Heraclides was to be our rendezvous upon the moon.

I may say that I had been somewhat familiar with the scenery of this part of the lunar world, for I had often studied it from the earth with a telescope, and I had thought that if there was any part of the moon where one might, with fair expectation of success, look for inhabitants, or if not for inhabitants, at least for relics of life no longer existent there, this would surely be the place. It was, therefore, with no small degree of curiosity, notwithstanding the unexpectedly frightful and repulsive appearance that the surface of the moon presented, that I now saw myself rapidly approaching the region concerning whose secrets my imagination had so often busied itself. When Mr. Edison and I had paid our previous visit to the moon on the first experimental trip of the electrical ship, we had landed at a point on its surface remote from this, and, as I have before explained, we then made no effort to investigate its secrets. But now it was to be different, and we were at length to see something of the wonders of the moon.

Like a Human Face.

I had often on the earth drawn a smile from my friends by showing them Cape Heraclides with a telescope, and calling their attention to the fact that the outline of the peak terminating the cape was such as to present a remarkable resemblance to a human face, unmistakably a feminine countenance, seen in profile, and possessing no small degree of beauty. To my astonishment, this curious human semblance still remained when we had approached so close to the moon that the mountains forming the cape filled nearly the whole field of view of the window from which I was watching it. The resemblance, indeed, was most startling.

The Resemblance Disappears.

"Can this indeed be Diana herself?" I said half aloud, but instantly afterward I was laughing at my fancy, for Mr. Edison had overheard me and exclaimed, "Where is she?"

"Who?"

"Diana."

"Why, there," I said, pointing to the moon. But lo! the appearance was gone even while I spoke. A swift change had taken place in the line of sight by which we were viewing it, and the likeness had disappeared in consequence.

A few moments later my astonishment was revived, but the cause this time was a very different one. We had been dropping rapidly toward the mountains, and the electrician in charge of the car was swiftly and constantly changing his potential, and, like a pilot who feels his way into an unknown harbor, endeavoring to approach the moon in such a manner that no hidden peril should surprise us. As we thus approached I suddenly perceived, crowning the very apex of the lofty peak near the termination of the cape, the ruins of what appeared to be an ancient watch tower. It was evidently composed of Cyclopean blocks larger than any that I had ever seen even among the ruins of Greece, Egypt and Asia Minor.

A Wonderful Discovery on the Moon!

As we thus approached I suddenly perceived, crowning the very apex of the lofty peak near the termination of the cape, the ruins of what appeared to be the ancient watch-tower.

The Moon Was Inhabited.

Here, then, was visible proof that the moon had been inhabited, although probably it was not inhabited now. I cannot describe the exultant feeling which took possession of me at this discovery. It settled so much that learned men had been disputing about for centuries.

"What will they say," I exclaimed, "when I show them a photograph of that?"

Below the peak, stretching far to right and left, lay a barren beach which had evidently once been washed by sea waves, because it was marked by long curved ridges such as the advancing and retiring tide leaves upon the shore of the ocean.

This beach sloped rapidly outward and downward toward a profound abyss, which had once, evidently, been the bed of a sea, but which now appeared to us simply as the empty, yawning shell of an ocean that had long vanished.

It was with no small difficulty, and only after the expenditure of considerable time, that all the floating ships of the squadron were gradually brought to rest on this lone mountain top of the moon. In accordance with my request, Mr. Edison had the flagship moored in the interior of the great ruined watch tower that I have described. The other ships rested upon the slope of the mountain around us.

Although time pressed, for we knew that the safety of the earth depended upon our promptness in attacking Mars, yet it was determined to remain here at least two or three days in order that the wrecked car might be repaired. It was found also that the passage of the highly electrified meteor had disarranged the electrical machinery in some of the other cars, so that there were many repairs to be made besides those needed to restore the wreck.

Burying the Dead.

Moreover, we must bury our unfortunate companions who had been killed by the meteor. This, in fact, was the first work that we performed. Strange was the sight, and stranger our feelings, as here on the surface of a world distant from the earth, and on soil which had never before been pressed by the foot of man, we performed that last ceremony of respect which mortals pay to mortality. In the ancient beach at the foot of the peak we made a deep opening, and there covered forever the faces of our friends, leaving them to sleep among the ruins of empires, and among the graves of races which had vanished probably ages before Adam and Eve appeared in Paradise.

While the repairs were being made several scientific expeditions were sent out in various directions across the moon. One went westward to investigate the great ring plain of Plato, and the lunar Alps. Another crossed the ancient Sea of Showers toward the lunar Apennines.

One started to explore the immense crater of Copernicus, which, yawning fifty miles across, presents a wonderful appearance even from the distance of the earth. The ship in which I, myself, had the good fortune to embark, was bound for the mysterious lunar mountain Aristarchus.

Before these expeditions started, a careful exploration had been made in the neighborhood of Cape Heraclides. But, except that the broken walls of the watch tower on the peak, composed of blocks of enormous size, had evidently been the work of creatures endowed with human intelligence, no remains were found indicating the former presence of inhabitants upon this part of the moon.

A Gigantic Human Footprint.

But along the shore of the old sea, just where the so-called Bay of Rainbows separates itself from the abyss of the Sea of Showers, there were found some stratified rocks in which the fascinated eyes of the explorer beheld the clear imprint of a gigantic human foot, measuring five feet in length from toe to heel.

Monsters Had Populated the Satellite.

The fascinated eyes of the explorer beheld the clear imprint of a gigantic human foot, measuring five feet in length from toe to heel.

Detailing the Marvellous Adventures of the Earth's Warriors in Unknown Worlds.

The most minute search failed to reveal another trace of the presence of the ancient giant, who had left the impress of his foot in the wet sands of the beach here so many millions of years ago that even the imagination of the geologists shrank from the task of attempting to fix the precise period.

The Great Footprint.

Around this gigantic footprint gathered most of the scientific members of the expedition, wearing their oddly shaped air-tight suits, connected with telephonic wires, and the spectacle, but for the impressiveness of the discovery, would have been laughable in the extreme. Bending over the mark in the rock, nodding their heads together, pointing with their awkwardly accoutred arms, they looked like an assemblage of antediluvian monsters collected around their prey. Their disappointment over the fact that no other marks of anything resembling human habitation could be discovered was very great.

Still this footprint in itself was quite sufficient, as they all declared, to settle the question of the former inhabitation of the moon, and it would serve for the production of many a learned volume after their return to the earth, even if no further discoveries should be made in other parts of the lunar world.

Expeditions Over the Moon.

It was the hope of making such other discoveries that led to the dispatch of the other various expeditions which I have already named. I had chosen to accompany the car that was going to Aristarchus, because, as every one who had viewed the moon from the earth was aware, there was something very mysterious about that mountain. I knew that it was a crater nearly thirty miles in diameter and very deep, although its floor was plainly visible.

The Glowing Mountains.

What rendered it remarkable was the fact that the floor and the walls of the crater, particularly on the inner side, glowed with a marvellous brightness which rendered them almost blinding when viewed with a powerful telescope.

So bright were they, indeed, that the eye was unable to see many of the details which the telescope would have made visible but for the flood of light which poured from the mountains. Sir William Herschel had been so completely misled by this appearance that he supposed he was watching a lunar volcano in eruption.

It had always been a difficult question what caused the extraordinary luminosity of Aristarchus. No end of hypotheses had been invented to account for it. Now I was to assist in settling these questions forever.

From Cape Heraclides to Aristarchus the distance in an air line was something over 300 miles. Our course lay across the northeastern part of the Sea of Showers, with enormous cliffs, mountain masses and peaks shining on the right, while in the other direction the view was bounded by the distant range of the lunar Apennines, some of whose towering peaks, when viewed from our immense elevation, appeared as sharp as the Swiss Matterhorn.

When we had arrived within about a hundred miles of our destination we found ourselves floating directly over the so-called Harbinger Mountains. The serrated peaks of Aristarchus then appeared ahead of us, fairly blazing in the sunshine.

A Gigantic String Of Diamonds.

It seemed as if a gigantic string of diamonds, every one as great as a mountain peak, had been cast down upon the barren surface of the moon and left to waste their brilliance upon the desert air of this abandoned world.

The Diamond Mountains of the Moon.

It seemed as if a gigantic string of diamonds, every one as great as a mountain, had been cast down upon the barren surface of the moon.

As we rapidly approached, the dazzling splendor of the mountain became almost unbearable to our eyes, and we were compelled to resort to the device, practiced by all climbers of lofty mountains, where the glare of sunlight upon snow surfaces is liable to cause temporary blindness, of protecting our eyes with neutral-tinted glasses.

Professor Moissan, the great French chemist and maker of artificial diamonds, fairly danced with delight.

"Voila! Voila! Voila!" was all that he could say.

A Mountain of Crystals.

When we were comparatively near, the mountain no longer seemed to glow with a uniform radiance, evenly distributed over its entire surface, but now innumerable points of light, all as bright as so many little suns, blazed away at us. It was evident that we had before us a mountain composed of, or at least covered with, crystals.

Without stopping to alight on the outer slopes of the great ring-shaped range of peaks which composed Aristarchus, we sailed over their rim and looked down into the interior. Here the splendor of the crystals was greater than on the outer slopes, and the broad floor of the crater, thousands of feet beneath us, shone and sparkled with overwhelming radiance, as if it were an immense bin of diamonds, while a peak in the centre flamed like a stupendous tiara incrusted with selected gems.

Eager to see what these crystals were, the car was now allowed rapidly to drop into the interior of the crater. With great caution we brought it to rest upon the blazing ground, for the sharp edges of the crystals would certainly have torn the metallic sides of the car if it had come into violent contact with them.

Donning our air-tight suits and stepping carefully out upon this wonderful footing we attempted to detach some of the crystals. Many of them were firmly fastened, but a few—some of astonishing size—were readily loosened.

A Wealth of Gems.

A moment's inspection showed that we had stumbled upon the most marvellous work of the forces of crystallization that human eyes had ever rested upon. Some time in the past history of the moon there had been an enormous outflow of molten material from the crater. This had overspread the walls and partially filled up the interior, and later its surface had flowered into gems, as thick as blossoms in a bed of pansies.

The whole mass flashed prismatic rays of indescribable beauty and intensity. We gazed at first speechless with amazement.

"It cannot be, surely it cannot be," said Professor Moissan at length.

"But it is," said another member of the party.

"Are these diamonds?" asked a third.

"I cannot yet tell," replied the Professor. "They have the brilliancy of diamonds, but they may be something else."

"Moon jewels," suggested a third.

"And worth untold millions, whatever they are," remarked another.

Jewels from the Moon.

These magnificent crystals, some of which appeared to be almost flawless, varied in size from the dimensions of a hazelnut to geometrical solids several inches in diameter. We carefully selected as many as it was convenient to carry and placed them in the car for future examination. We had solved another long standing lunar problem and had, perhaps, opened up an inexhaustible mine of wealth which might eventually go far toward reimbursing the earth for the damage which it had suffered from the invasion of the Martians.

On returning to Cape Heraclides we found that the other expeditions had arrived at the rendezvous ahead of us. Their members had wonderful stories to tell of what they had seen, but nothing caused quite so much astonishment as that which we had to tell and to show.

The party which had gone to visit Plato and the lunar Alps brought back, however, information which, in a scientific sense, was no less interesting than what we had been able to gather.

They had found within this curious ring of Plato, which is a circle of mountains sixty miles in diameter, enclosing a level plain remarkably smooth over most of its surface, unmistakable evidences of former inhabitation. A gigantic city had evidently at one time existed near the centre of this great plain. The outlines of its walls and the foundation marks of some of its immense buildings were plainly made out, and elaborate plans of this vanished capital of the moon were prepared by several members of the party.

More Evidences of Habitation.

One of them was fortunate enough to discover an even more precious relic of the ancient lunarians. It was a piece of petrified skullbone, representing but a small portion of the head to which it had belonged, but yet sufficient to enable the anthropologists, who immediately fell to examining it, to draw ideal representations of the head as it must have been in life—the head of a giant of enormous size, which, if it had possessed a highly organized brain, of proportionate magnitude, must have given to its possessor intellectual powers immensely greater than any of the descendants of Adam have ever been endowed with.

Giants in Size.

Indeed, one of the professors was certain that some little concretions found on the interior of the piece of skull were petrified portions of the brain matter itself, and he set to work with the microscope to examine its organic quality.

In the mean time, the repairs to the electrical ships had been completed, and, although these discoveries upon the moon had created a most profound sensation among the members of the expedition, and aroused an almost irresistible desire to continue the explorations thus happily begun, yet everybody knew that these things were aside from the main purpose in view, and that we should be false to our duty in wasting a moment more upon the moon than was absolutely necessary to put the ships in proper condition to proceed on their warlike voyage.

Departing from the Moon.

Everything being prepared then, we left the moon with great regret, just forty-eight hours after we had landed upon its surface, carrying with us a determination to revisit it and to learn more of its wonderful secrets in case we should survive the dangers which we were now going to face.

Chapter VI

A day or two after leaving the moon we had another adventure with a wandering inhabitant of space which brought us into far greater peril than had our encounter with the meteor.

The airships had been partitioned off so that a portion of the interior could be darkened in order to serve as a sleeping chamber, wherein, according to the regulations prescribed by the commander of the squadron each member of the expedition in his turn passed eight out of every twenty-four hours—sleeping if he could, if not, meditating, in a more or less dazed way, upon the wonderful things that he was seeing and doing—things far more incredible than the creations of a dream.

One morning, if I may call by the name morning the time of my periodical emergence from the darkened chamber, glancing from one of the windows, I was startled to see in the black sky a brilliant comet.

The Adventure With The Comet.

A Thrilling Story of an Encounter that Nearly Ended the Great Expedition.

No periodical comet, as I knew, was at this time approaching the neighborhood of the sun, and no stranger of that kind had been detected from the observatories making its way sunward before we left the earth. Here, however, was unmistakably a comet rushing toward the sun, flinging out a great gleaming tail behind it and so close to us that I wondered to see it remaining almost motionless in the sky. This phenomenon was soon explained to me, and the explanation was of a most disquieting character.

The stranger had already been perceived, not only from the flagship, but from the other members of the squadron, and, as I now learned, efforts had been made to get out of the neighborhood, but for some reason the electrical apparatus did not work perfectly—some mysterious disturbing force acting upon it—and so it had been found impossible to avoid an encounter with the comet, not an actual coming into contact with it, but a falling into the sphere of its influence.

In the Wake of the Comet.

In fact, I was informed that for several hours the squadron had been dragging along in the wake of a comet, very much as boats are sometimes towed off by a wounded whale. Every effort had been made to so adjust the electric charge upon the ships that they would be repelled from the cometic mass, but, owing apparently to eccentric changes continually going on in the electric charge affecting the clashing mass of meteoric bodies which constituted the head of the comet, we found it impossible to escape from its influence.

At one instant the ships would be repelled; immediately afterward they would be attracted again, and thus they were dragged hither and thither, but never able to break from the invisible leash which the comet had cast upon them. The latter was moving with enormous velocity toward the sun, and, consequently, we were being carried back again, away from the object of our expedition, with a fair prospect of being dissipated in blazing vapors when the comet had dragged us, unwilling prisoners, into the immediate neighborhood of the solar furnace.

Even the most cool-headed lost his self-control in this terrible emergency. Every kind of device that experience or the imagination could suggest was tried, but nothing would do. Still on we rushed with the electrified atoms composing the tail of the comet sweeping to and fro over the members of the squadron, as they shifted their position, like the plume of smoke from a gigantic steamer, drifting over the sea birds that follow in its course.

Is This the End?

Was this to end it all, then? Was this the fate that Providence had in store for us? Were the hopes of the earth thus to perish? Was the expedition to be wrecked and its fate to remain forever unknown to the planet from which it had set forth? And was our beloved globe, which had seemed so fair to us when we last looked upon it near by, and in whose defence we had resolved to spend our last breath, to be left helpless and at the mercy of its implacable foe in the sky?

In the Power of a Great Comet.

Was This to End It All, Then? Was This the Fate That Providence Had In Store for Us? Was the Expedition to Be Exterminated?

At length we gave ourselves up for lost. There seemed to be no possible way to free ourselves from the baleful grip of this terrible and unlooked-for enemy.

Giving Up All Hope.

As the comet approached the sun its electric energy rapidly increased, and watching it with telescopes, for we could not withdraw our fascinated eyes from it, we could clearly behold the fearful things that went on in its nucleus.

This consisted of an immense number of separate meteors of no very great size individually, but which were in constant motion among one another, darting to and fro, clashing and smashing together, while fountains of blazing metallic particles and hot mineral vapors poured out in every direction.

A Flying Hell.

As I watched it, unable to withdraw my eyes, I saw imaginary forms revealing themselves amid the flaming meteors. They seemed like creatures in agony, tossing their arms, bewailing in their attitudes the awful fate that had overtaken them, and fairly chilling my blood with the pantomime of torture which they exhibited. I thought of an old superstition which I had often heard about the earth, and exclaimed: "Yes, surely, this is a flying hell!"

As the electric activity of the comet increased, its continued changes of potential and polarity became more frequent, and the electrical ships darted about with even greater confusion than before. Occasionally one of them, seized with a sudden impulse, would spring forward toward the nucleus of the comet with a sudden access of velocity that would fling every one of its crew from his feet, and all would lie sprawling on the floor of the car while it rushed, as it seemed, to inevitable and instant destruction.

Saved on Ruin's Brink.

Then, either through the frantic efforts of the electrician struggling with the controller or through another change in the polarity of the comet, the ship would be saved on the very brink of ruin and stagger away out of immediate danger.

Thus the captured squadron was swept, swaying and darting hither and thither, but never able to get sufficiently far from the comet to break the bond of its fatal attraction.

The Earth Again!

So great was our excitement and so complete our absorption in the fearful peril that we had not noticed the precise direction in which the comet was carrying us. It was enough to know that the goal of the journey was the furnace of the sun. But presently someone in the flagship recalled us to a more accurate sense of our situation in space by exclaiming:

"Why, there is the earth!"

Thrilling Adventures Crowd Each Other In the Great War Upon Mars.

And there, indeed, it was, its great globe rolling under our eyes, with the contrasted colors of the continents and clouds and the watery gleam of the ocean spread beneath us.

"We are going to strike it!" exclaimed somebody. "The comet is going to dash into the earth."

Such a collision at first seemed inevitable, but presently it was noticed that the direction of the comet's motion was such that while it might graze the earth it would not actually strike it.

And so, like a swarm of giant insects circling about an electric light from whose magic influence they cannot escape, our ships went on, to be whipped against the earth in passing and then to continue their swift journey to destruction.

Unexpected Aid.

"Thank God, this saves us," suddenly cried Mr. Edison.

"What—what?"

"Why, the earth, of course. Do you not see that as the comet sweeps close to the great planet the superior attraction of the latter will snatch us from its grasp, and that thus we shall be able to escape?"

And it was indeed as Mr. Edison had predicted. In a blaze of falling meteors the comet swept the outer limits of the earth's atmosphere and passed on, while the swaying ships, having been instructed by signals what to do, desperately applied their electrical machinery to reverse the attraction and threw themselves into the arms of their mother earth.

Over the Atlantic.

In another instant we were all free, settling down through the quiet atmosphere with the Atlantic Ocean sparkling in the morning sun far below.

We looked at one another in amazement. So this was the end of our voyage! This was the completion of our warlike enterprise. We had started out to conquer a world, and we had come back ignominiously dragged in the train of a comet.

The earth which we were going to defend and protect had herself turned protector, and reaching out her strong arm had snatched her foolish children from the destruction which they had invited.

It would be impossible to describe the chagrin of every member of the expedition.

A Feeling of Shame.

The electric ships rapidly assembled and hovered high in the air, while their commanders consulted about what should be done. A universal feeling of shame almost drove them to a decision not to land upon the surface of the planet, and if possible not to let its inhabitants know what had occurred.

But it was too late for that. Looking carefully beneath us, we saw that fate had brought us back to our very starting point, and signals displayed in the neighborhood of New York indicated that we had already been recognized. There was nothing for us then but to drop down and explain the situation.

I shall not delay my narrative by undertaking to describe the astonishment and the disappointment of the inhabitants of the earth when, within a fortnight from our departure, they saw us back again, with no laurels of victory crowning our brows.

At first they had hoped that we were returning in triumph, and we were overwhelmed with questions the moment we had dropped within speaking distance.

"Have you whipped them?"

"How many are lost?"

"Is there any more danger?"

"Faix, have ye got one of thim men from Mars?"

But their rejoicings and their facetiousness were turned into wailing when the truth was imparted.

A Short Stay on the Earth.

We made a short story of it, for we had not the heart to go into details. We told of our unfortunate comrades whom we had buried on the moon, and there was one gleam of satisfaction when we exhibited the wonderful crystals we had collected in the crater of Aristarchus.

Mr. Edison determined to stop only long enough to test the electrical machinery of the cars, which had been more or less seriously deranged during our wild chase after the comet, and then to start straight back for Mars—this time on a through trip.

Mysterious Lights on Mars.

The astronomers, who had been watching Mars, since our departure, with their telescopes, reported that mysterious lights continued to be visible, but that nothing indicating the starting of another expedition for the earth had been seen.

Within twenty-four hours we were ready for our second start.

The moon was now no longer in a position to help us on our way. It had moved out of the line between Mars and the earth.

High above us, in the centre of the heavens, glowed the red planet which was the goal of our journey.

The needed computations of velocity and direction of flight having been repeated, and the ships being all in readiness, we started direct for Mars.

Greater Preparations Made.

An enormous charge of electricity was imparted to each member of the squadron, in order that as soon as we had reached the upper limits of the atmosphere, where the ships could move swiftly, without danger of being consumed by the heat developed by the friction of their passage through the air, a very great initial velocity could be imparted.

Once started off by this tremendous electrical kick, and with no atmosphere to resist our motion, we should be able to retain the same velocity, barring incidental encounters, until we arrived near the surface of Mars.

When we were free of the atmosphere, and the ships were moving away from the earth, with the highest velocity which we were able to impart to them, observations on the stars were made in order to determine the rate of our speed.

Ten Miles A Second!

This was found to be ten miles in a second, or 864,000 miles in a day, a very much greater speed than that with which we had travelled on starting to touch at the moon. Supposing this velocity to remain uniform, and, with no known resistance, it might reasonably be expected to do so, we should arrive at Mars in a little less than forty-two days, the distance of the planet from the earth being, at this time, about thirty-six million miles.

Nothing occurred for many days to interrupt our journey. We became accustomed to our strange surroundings, and many entertainments were provided to while away the time. The astronomers in the expedition found plenty of occupation in studying the aspects of the stars and the other heavenly bodies from their new point of view.

Drawing Near to Mars.

At the expiration of about thirty-five days we had drawn so near to Mars that with our telescopes, which, though small, were of immense power, we could discern upon its surface features and details which no one had been able to glimpse from the earth.

As the surface of this world, that we were approaching as a tiger hunter draws near the jungle, gradually unfolded itself to our inspection, there was hardly one of us willing to devote to sleep or idleness the prescribed eight hours that had been fixed as the time during which each member of the expedition must remain in the darkened chamber. We were too eager to watch for every new revelation upon Mars.

But something was in store that we had not expected. We were to meet the Martians before arriving at the world they dwelt in.

Among the stars which shone in that quarter of the heavens where Mars appeared as the master orb, there was one, lying directly in our path, which, to our astonishment, as we continued on, altered from the aspect of a star, underwent a gradual magnification, and soon presented itself in the form of a little planet.

The Asteroid.

"It is an asteroid," said somebody.

"Yes, evidently; but how does it come inside the orbit of Mars?"

"Oh, there are several asteroids," said one of the astronomers, "which travel inside the orbit of Mars, along a part of their course, and, for aught we can tell, there may be many which have not yet been caught sight of from the earth, that are nearer to the sun than Mars is."

"This must be one of them."

"Manifestly so."

As we drew nearer the mysterious little planet revealed itself to us as a perfectly formed globe not more than five miles in diameter.

Approaching the Great Asteroid.

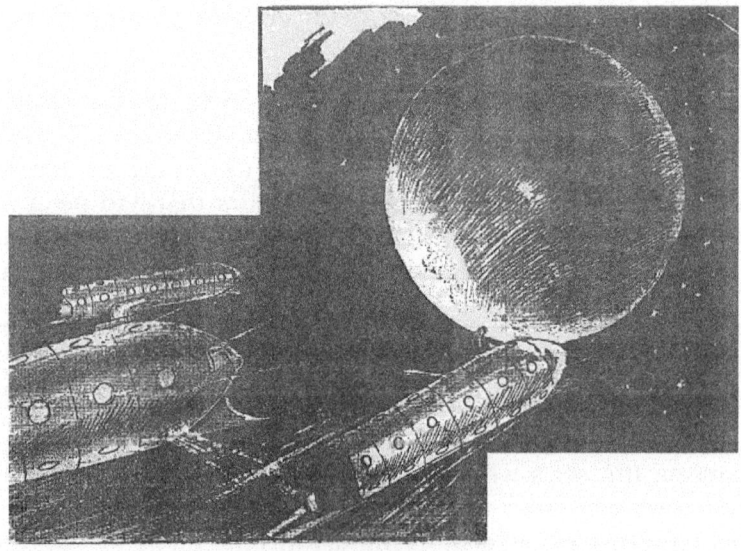

It altered from the aspect of a star, underwent a gradual magnification, and soon presented itself in the form of a little planet.

"What is that upon it?" asked Lord Kelvin, squinting intently at the little world through his glass. "As I live, it moves."

A Martian Appears!

The First Glimpse of the Horrible Inhabitants of the Red Planet.

"Yes, yes!" exclaimed several others, "there are inhabitants upon it, but what giants!"

"What monsters!"

"Don't you see?" exclaimed an excited savant. "They are the Martians!"

The startling truth burst upon the minds of all. Here upon this little planetoid were several of the gigantic inhabitants of the world that we were going to attack. There was more than one man in the flagship who recognized them well, and who shuddered at the recognition, instinctively recalling the recent terrible experience of the earth.

The Martian, Terrible to Behold!

Like men, and yet not like men; combining the human and the beast in their appearance, it required a steady nerve to look at them.... In our eyes their moral character shone through their physical aspect and thus rendered them more terrible!

Was this an outpost of the warlike Mars?

Around these monstrous enemies we saw several of their engines of war. Some of these appeared to have been wrecked, but at least one, as far as we could see, was still in a proper condition for use.

How had these creatures got there?

"Why, that is easy enough to account for," I said, as a sudden recollection flashed into my mind. "Don't you remember the report of the astronomers more than six months ago, at the end of the conference in Washington, that something would seem to indicate the departure of a new expedition from Mars had been noticed by them? We have heard nothing of that expedition since. We know that it did not reach the earth. It must have fallen foul of this asteroid, run upon this rock in the ocean of space and been wrecked here."

"We've got 'em, then," shouted our electric steersman, who had been a workman in Mr. Edison's laboratory and had unlimited confidence in his chief.

Preparing to Land.

The electrical ships were immediately instructed by signal to slow down, an operation that was easily affected through the electrical repulsion of the asteroid.

The nearer we got the more terrifying was the appearance of the gigantic creatures who were riding upon the little world before us like castaway sailors upon a block of ice. Like men, and yet not like men, combining the human and the beast in their appearance, it required a steady nerve to look at them. If we had not known their malignity and their power to work evil, it would have been different, but in our eyes their moral character shone through their physical aspect and thus rendered them more terrible than they would otherwise have been.

The Martians Recognize Us.

When we first saw them their appearance was most forlorn, and their attitudes indicated only despair and desperation, but as they caught sight of us their malign power of intellect instantly penetrated the mystery, and they recognized us for what we were.

Their despair immediately gave place to reawakened malevolence. On the instant they were astir, with such heart-chilling movements as those that characterize a venomous serpent preparing to strike.

Not imagining that they would be in a position to make serious resistance, we had been somewhat incautious in approaching.

The Awful Heat Ray.

Suddenly there was a quicker movement than usual among the Martians, a swift adjustment of that one of their engines of war which, as already noticed, seemed to be practically uninjured, and then there darted from it and alighted upon one of the foremost ships a dazzling lightning stroke a mile in length, at whose touch the metallic sides of the car curled and withered and, licked for a moment by what seemed lambent flames, collapsed into a mere cinder.

Another Ship Destroyed.

The Death-Dealing Martians Strike a Fearful Blow at the Earth's Warriors.

For an instant not a word was spoken, so sudden and unexpected was the blow.

We knew that every soul in the stricken car had perished.

"Back! Back!" was the signal instantaneously flashed from the flagship, and reversing their polarities the members of the squadron sprang away from the little planet as rapidly as the electrical impulse could drive them.

But before we were out of reach a second flaming tongue of death shot from the fearful engine, and another of our ships, with all its crew, was destroyed.

The Terrible Work of the Martians' All-Powerful Fire-Blast.

"Back! Back!" was the signal instantaneously flashed from the flag ship, and the members of the squadron sprang away from the little planet. But before we were out of reach a second tongue of death shot from the fearful engine, and another of our ships, with all of its crew, was destroyed.

A Discouraging Beginning.

It was an inauspicious beginning for us. Two of our electrical ships, with their entire crews, had been wiped out of existence, and this appalling blow had been dealt by a few stranded and disabled enemies floating on an asteroid.

What hope would there be for us when we came to encounter the millions of Mars itself on their own ground and prepared for war?

However, it would not do to despond. We had been incautious, and we should take good care not to commit the same fault again.

Vengeance the First Thing!

The first thing to do was to avenge the death of our comrades. The question whether we were able to meet these Martians and overcome them might as well be settled right here and now. They had proved what they could do, even when disabled and at a disadvantage. Now it was our turn.

Chapter VII

The squadron had been rapidly withdrawn to a very considerable distance from the asteroid. The range of the mysterious artillery employed by the Martians was unknown to us. We did not even know the limit of the effective range of our own disintegrators. If it should prove that the Martians were able to deal their strokes at a distance greater than any we could reach, then they would of course have an insuperable advantage.

On the other hand, if it should turn out that our range was greater than theirs, the advantage would be on our side. Or—which was perhaps most probable—there might be practically no difference in the effective range of the engines.

Anyhow, we were going to find out how the case stood, and that without delay.

Ready with the Disintegrator.

Everything being in readiness, the disintegrators all in working order, and the men who were able to handle them, most of whom were experienced marksmen, chosen from among the officers of the regular army of the United States, and accustomed to the straight shooting and the sure hits of the West, standing at their posts, the squadron again advanced.

In order to distract the attention of the Martians, the electrical ships had been distributed over a wide space. Some dropped straight down toward the asteroid; others approached it by flank attack, from this side and that. The flagship moved straight in toward the point where the first disaster occurred. Its intrepid commander felt that his post should be that of the greatest danger, and where the severest blows would be given and received.

A Strategic Advance.

The approach of the ships was made with great caution. Watching the Martians with our telescopes we could clearly see that they were disconcerted by the scattered order of our attack. Even if all of their engines of war had been in proper condition for use it would have been impossible for them to meet the simultaneous assault of so many enemies dropping down upon them from the sky.

But they were made of fighting metal, as we knew from old experience. It was no question of surrender. They did not know how to surrender, and we did not know how to demand a surrender. Besides, the destruction of the two electrical ships with the forty men, many of whom bore names widely known upon the earth, had excited a kind of fury among the members of the squadron which called for vengeance.

Another Attack.

Suddenly a repetition of the quick movement by the Martians, which had been the forerunner of the former coup, was observed; again a blinding flash burst from their war engine and instantaneously a shiver ran through the frame of the flagship; the air within quivered with strange pulsations and seemed suddenly to have assumed the temperature of a blast furnace.

We all gasped for breath. Our throats and lungs seemed scorched in the act of breathing. Some fell unconscious upon the floor. The marksmen, carrying the disintegrators ready for use, staggered, and one of them dropped his instrument.

But we had not been destroyed like our comrades before us. In a moment the wave of heat passed; those who had fallen recovered from their momentary stupor and staggered to their feet.

The electrical steersman stood hesitating at his post.

"Move on," said Mr. Edison sternly, his features set with determination and his eyes afire. "We are still beyond their effective range. Let us get closer in order to make sure work when we strike."

The ship moved on. One could hear the heartbeats of its inmates. The other members of the squadron, thinking for the moment that disaster had overtaken the flagship, had paused and seemed to be meditating flight.

"Signal them to move on," said Mr. Edison.

The Battle Commences.

The signal was given, and the circle of electrical ships closed in upon the asteroid.

In the meantime Mr. Edison had been donning his air-tight suit. Before we could clearly comprehend his intention he had passed through the double-trapped door which gave access to the exterior of the car without permitting the loss of air, and was standing upon what served as the deck of the ship.

In his hand he carried a disintegrator. With a quick motion he sighted it.

As quickly as possible I sprang to his side. I was just in time to note the familiar blue gleam about the instrument, which indicated that its terrific energies were at work. The whirring sound was absent, because here, in open space, where there was no atmosphere, there could be no sound.

The Disintegrator's Power.

My eyes were fixed upon the Martians' engine, which had just dealt us a staggering, but not fatal, blow, and particularly I noticed a polished knob projecting from it, which seemed to have been the focus from which its destructive bolt emanated.

A moment later the knob disappeared. The irresistible vibrations darted from the electrical disintegrator and had fallen upon it and instantaneously shattered it into atoms.

"That fixes them," said Mr. Edison, turning to me with a smile.

And indeed it did fix them. We had most effectually spiked their gun. It would deal no more death blows.

The doings of the flagship had been closely watched throughout the squadron. The effect of its blow had been evident to all, and a moment later we saw, on some of the nearer ships, men dressed in their air suits, appearing upon the deck, swinging their arms and sending forth noiseless cheers into empty space.

A Telling Stroke.

The stroke that we had dealt was taken by several of the electrical ships as a signal for a common assault, and we saw two of the Martians fall beside the ruin of their engine, their heads having been blown from their bodies.

"Signal them to stop firing," commanded Mr. Edison. "We have got them down, and we are not going to murder them without necessity."

"Besides," he added, "I want to capture some of them alive."

The signal was given as he had ordered. The flagship then alone dropped slowly toward the place on the asteroid where the prostrate Martians were.

A Terrible Scene.

As we got near them a terrible scene unfolded itself to our eyes. There had evidently been not more than half a dozen of the monsters in the beginning. Two of these were stretched headless upon the ground. Three others had suffered horrible injuries where the invisible vibratory beams from the disintegrators had grazed them, and they could not long survive. One only remained apparently uninjured.

Vengeance at Last Upon the Pitiless Martians.

As we got near them a terrible scene unfolded itself. Two of the Martians were stretched headless upon the ground. Three others had suffered horrible injuries, and only one remained unhurt.

The Gigantic Martian.

It is impossible for me to describe the appearance of this creature in terms that would be readily understood. Was he like a man? Yes and no. He possessed many human characteristics, but they were exaggerated and monstrous in scale and in detail. His head was of enormous size, and his huge projecting eyes gleamed with a strange fire of intelligence. His face was like a caricature, but not one to make the beholder laugh. Drawing himself up, he towered to a height of at least fifteen feet.

But let the reader not suppose from this inadequate description that the Martians stirred in the beholder precisely the sensation that would be caused by the sight of a gorilla, or other repulsive inhabitant of one of our terrestrial jungles, suddenly confronting him in its native wilds.

With all his horrible characteristics, and all his suggestions of beast and monster, nevertheless the Martian produced the impression of being a person and not a mere animal.

His Frightened Aspect.

I have already referred to the enormous size of his head, and to the fact that his countenance bore considerable resemblance to that of a man. There was something in this face that sent a shiver through the soul of the beholder. One could feel in looking upon it that here was intellect, intelligence developed to the highest degree, but in the direction of evil instead of good.

The sensations of one who had stood face to face with Satan, when he was driven from the battlements of heaven by the swords of his fellow archangels, and had beheld him transformed from Lucifer, the Son of the Morning, into the Prince of Night and Hell, might not have been unlike those which we now experienced as we gazed upon this dreadful personage, who seemed to combine the intellectual powers of a man, raised to their highest pitch, with some of the physical features of a beast, and all the moral depravity of a fiend.

The Martian's Rage.

The appearance of the Martian was indeed so threatening and repellent that we paused at the height of fifty feet above the ground, hesitating to approach nearer. A grin of rage and hate overspread his face. If he had been a man I should say he shook his fist at us. What he did was to express in even more telling pantomime his hatred and defiance, and his determination to grind us to shreds if he could once get us within his clutches.

Mr. Edison and I still stood upon the deck of the ship, where several others had gathered around us. The atmosphere of the little asteroid was so rare that it practically amounted to nothing, and we could not possibly have survived if we had not continued to wear our air-tight suits. How the Martians contrived to live here was a mystery to us. It was another of their secrets which we were yet to learn.

Mr. Edison retained his disintegrator in his hand.

"Kill him," said someone. "He is too horrible to live."

"If we do not kill him we shall never be able to land upon the asteroid," said another.

Shall We Kill Him?

"No," said Mr. Edison, "I shall not kill him. We have got another use for him. Tom," he continued, turning to one of his assistants, whom he had brought from his laboratory, "bring me the anaesthetizer."

This was something entirely new to nearly all the members of the expedition. Mr. Edison, however, had confided to me before we left the earth the fact that he had invented a little instrument by means of which a bubble, strongly charged with a powerful anaesthetic agent, could be driven to a considerable distance into the face of an enemy, where, exploding without other damage, it would instantly put him to sleep.

When Tom had placed the instrument in his hands Mr. Edison ordered the electrical ship to forge slightly ahead and drop a little lower toward the Martian, who, with watchful eyes and threatening gestures, noted our approach in the attitude of a wild beast on the spring. Suddenly Mr. Edison discharged from the instrument in his hand a little gaseous globe, which glittered like a ball of tangled rainbows in the sunshine, and darted with astonishing velocity straight into the upturned face of the Martian. It burst as it touched and the monster fell back senseless upon the ground.

One of the Bellicose Martians Falls Into the Hands of the Worldians.

"You have killed him!" exclaimed all.

"No," said Mr. Edison, "he is not dead, only asleep. Now we shall drop down and bind him tight before he can awake."

When we came to bind our prisoner with strong ropes we were more than ever impressed with his gigantic stature and strength. Evidently in single combat with equal weapons he would have been a match for twenty of us.

A Gigantic Martian Captured.

When we came to bind our prisoner with strong ropes we were more than ever impressed with his gigantic stature and strength. He might have been a match for twenty of us.

All that I had read of giants had failed to produce upon my mind the impression of enormous size and tremendous physical energy which the sleeping body of this immense Martian produced. He had fallen on his back, and was in a most profound slumber. All his features were relaxed, and yet even in that condition there was a devilishness about him that made the beholders instinctively shudder.

The Unconscious Martian.

So powerful was the effect of the anaesthetic which Mr. Edison had discharged into his face that he remained perfectly unconscious while we turned him half over in order the more securely to bind his muscular limbs.

In the meantime the other electrical ships approached, and several of them made a landing upon the asteroid. Everybody was eager to see this wonderful little world, which, as I have already remarked, was only five miles in diameter.

Exploring the Planet.

Several of us from the flagship started out hastily to explore the miniature planet. And now our attention was recalled to an intensely interesting phenomenon which had engaged our thoughts not only when we were upon the moon, but during our flight through space. This was the almost entire absence of weight.

On the moon, where the force of gravitation is one-sixth as great as upon the earth, we had found ourselves astonishingly light. Five-sixths of our own weight, and of the weight of the air-tight suits in which we were incased, had magically dropped from us. It was therefore comparatively easy for us, encumbered as we were, to make our way about on the moon.

But when we were far from both the earth and the moon, the loss of weight was more astonishing still—not astonishing because we had not known that it would be so, but nevertheless a surprising phenomenon in contrast with our lifelong experience on the earth.

Men Without Weight.

In open space we were practically without weight. Only the mass of the electrical car in which we were enclosed attracted us, and inside that we could place ourselves in any position without falling. We could float in the air. There were no up and no down, no top and no bottom for us. Stepping outside the car, it would have been easy for us to spring away from it and leave it forever.

One of the most startling experiences that I have ever had was one day when we were navigating space about half way between the earth and Mars. I had stepped outside the car with Lord

Kelvin, both of us, of course, wearing our air-tight suits. We were perfectly well aware what would be the consequence of detaching ourselves from the car as we moved along. We should still retain the forward motion of the car, and of course accompany it in its flight. There would be no falling one way or the other. The car would have a tendency to draw us back again by its attraction, but this tendency would be very slight, and practically inappreciable at a distance.

Stepping Into Space.

"I am going to step off," I suddenly said to Lord Kelvin. "Of course I shall keep right along with the car, and step aboard again when I am ready."

Stepping into Space Thousands of Miles from Land.

"I am going to step off," I suddenly said to Lord Kelvin.

"Quite right on general principles, young man," replied the great savant, "but beware in what manner you step off. Remember, if you give your body an impulse sufficient to carry it away from the car to any considerable distance, you will be unable to get back again, unless we can catch you with a boathook or a fishline. Out there in empty space you will have nothing to kick against, and you will be unable to propel yourself in the direction of the car, and its attraction is so feeble that we should probably arrive at Mars before it had drawn you back again."

All this was, of course, perfectly self-evident, yet I believe that but for the warning word of Lord Kelvin, I should have been rash enough to step out into empty space with sufficient force to have separated myself hopelessly from the electrical ship.

A Reckless Experiment.

As it was, I took good care to retain a hold upon a projecting portion of the car. Occasionally cautiously releasing my grip, I experienced for a few minutes the delicious, indescribable pleasure of being a little planet swinging through space, with nothing to hold me up and nothing to interfere with my motion.

Mr. Edison, happening to come upon the deck of the ship at this time, and seeing what we were about, at once said:

"I must provide against this danger. If I do not, there is a chance that we shall arrive at Mars with the ships half empty and the crews floating helplessly around us."

Edison Always Prepared.

Mr. Edison's way of guarding against the danger was by contriving a little apparatus, modeled after that which was the governing force of the electrical ships themselves, and which, being enclosed in the air-tight suits, enabled their wearers to manipulate the electrical charge upon them in such a way that they could make excursions from the cars into open space like steam launches from a ship, going and returning at their will.

These little machines being rapidly manufactured, for Mr. Edison had a miniature laboratory aboard, were distributed about the squadron, and henceforth we had the pleasure of paying and receiving visits among the various members of the fleet.

But to return from this digression to our experience of the asteroid. The latter being a body of some mass was, of course, able to impart to us a measurable degree of weight. Being five miles in diameter, on the assumption that its mean density was the same as that of the earth, the weight of bodies on its surface should have borne the same ratio to their weight upon the earth that the radius of the asteroid bore to the radius of the earth; in other words, as 1 to 1,600.

Having made this mental calculation, I knew that my weight, being 150 pounds on the earth, should on this asteroid be an ounce and a half.

Curious to see whether fact would bear out theory, I had myself weighed with a spring balance. Mr. Edison, Lord Kelvin and the other distinguished scientists stood by watching the operation with great interest.

To our complete surprise, my weight, instead of coming out an ounce and a half, as it should have done, on the supposition that the mean density of the asteroid resembled that of the earth—a very liberal supposition on the side of the asteroid, by the way—actually came out five ounces and a quarter!

"What in the world makes me so heavy?" I asked.

"Yes, indeed, what an elephant you have become," said Mr. Edison.

Lord Kelvin screwed his eyeglass in his eye, and carefully inspected the balance.

Weight, Five and a Quarter Ounces.

"It's quite right," he said. "You do indeed weigh five ounces and a quarter. Too much; altogether too much," he added. "You shouldn't do it, you know."

"Perhaps the fault is in the asteroid," suggested Professor Sylvanus P. Thompson.

"Quite so," exclaimed Lord Kelvin, a look of sudden comprehension overspreading his features. "No doubt it is the internal constitution of the asteroid which is the cause of the anomaly. We must look into that. Let me see? This gentleman's weight is three and one-half times as great as it ought to be. What element is there whose density exceeds the mean density of the earth in about that proportion?"

"Gold," exclaimed one of the party.

The Golden Asteroid!

For a moment we were startled beyond expression. The truth had flashed upon us.

This must be a golden planet—this little asteroid. If it were not composed internally of gold it could never have made me weigh three times more than I ought to weigh.

"But where is the gold?" cried one.

"Covered up, of course," said Lord Kelvin. "Buried in star dust. This asteroid could not have continued to travel for millions of years through regions of space strewn with meteoric particles without becoming covered with the inevitable dust and grime of such a journey. We must dig down, and then doubtless we shall find the metal."

This hint was instantly acted upon. Something that would serve for a spade was seized by one of the men, and in a few minutes a hole had been dug in the comparatively light soil of the asteroid.

The Precious Metal Discovered.

I shall never forget the sight, nor the exclamations of wonder that broke forth from all of us standing around, when the yellow gleam of the precious metal appeared under the "star dust." Collected in huge masses it reflected the light of the sun from its hiding place.

Evidently the planet was not a solid ball of gold, formed like a bullet run in a mould, but was composed of nuggets of various sizes, which had come together here under the influence of their mutual gravitation, and formed a little metallic planet.

Judging by the test of weight which we had already tried, and which had led to the discovery of the gold, the composition of the asteroid must be the same to its very centre.

An Incredible Phenomenon.

In an assemblage of famous scientific men such as this the discovery of course immediately led to questions as to the origin of this incredible phenomenon.

How did these masses of gold come together? How did it chance that, with the exception of the thin crust of the asteroid, nearly all its substance was composed of the precious metal?

One asserted that it was quite impossible that there should be so much gold at so great a distance from the sun.

"It is the general law," he said, "that the planets increase in density toward the sun. There is every reason to think that the inner planets possess the greater amount of dense elements, while the outer ones are comparatively light."

Whence Came the Treasure?

But another referred to the old theory that there was once in this part of the solar system a planet which had been burst in pieces by some mysterious explosion, the fragments forming what we know as the asteroids. In his opinion, this planet might have contained a large quantity of gold, and in the course of ages the gold, having, in consequence of its superior atomic weight, not being so widely scattered by the explosion as some of the other elements of the planet, had collected itself together in this body.

But I observed that Lord Kelvin and the other more distinguished men of science said nothing during this discussion. The truly learned man is the truly wise man. They were not going to set up theories without sufficient facts to sustain them. The one fact that the gold was here was all they had at present. Until they could learn more they were not prepared to theorize as to how the gold got there.

And in truth, it must be confessed, the greater number of us really cared less for the explanation of the wonderful fact than we did for the fact itself.

Gold is a thing which may make its appearance anywhere and at any time without offering any excuses or explanations.

Visions of Mighty Fortunes.

"Phew! Won't we be rich?" exclaimed a voice.

"How are we going to dig it and get it back to earth?" asked another.

"Carry it in your pockets," said one.

"No need of staking claims here," remarked another. "There is enough for everybody."

Mr. Edison suddenly turned the current of talk.

"What do you suppose those Martians were doing here?"

"Why, they were wrecked here."

"Not a bit of it," said Mr. Edison. "According to your own showing they could not have been wrecked here. This planet hasn't gravitation enough to wreck them by a fall, and besides I have been looking at their machines and I know there has been a fight."

"A fight?" exclaimed several, pricking up their ears.

"Yes," said Mr. Edison; "those machines bear the marks of the lightning of the Martians. They have been disabled, but they are made of some metal or some alloy of metals unknown to me, and consequently they have withstood the destructive force applied to them, as our electric ships were unable to withstand it. It is perfectly plain to me that they have been disabled in a battle. The Martians must have been fighting among themselves."

A Martian Civil War!

"About the gold!" exclaimed one.

"Of course. What else was there to fight about?"

At this instant one of our men came running from a considerable distance, waving his arms excitedly, but unable to give voice to his story, in the inappreciable atmosphere of the asteroid, until he had come up and made telephonic connection with us.

"There is a lot of dead Martians over there," he said. "They've been cleaning one another out."

"That's it," said Mr. Edison. "I knew it when I saw the condition of those machines."

"Then this is not a wrecked expedition, directed against the earth?"

"Not at all."

"This must be the great gold mine of Mars," said the president of an Australian mining company, opening both his eyes and his mouth as he spoke.

"Yes, evidently that's it. Here's where they come to get their wealth."

"And this," I said, "must be their harvest time. You notice that this asteroid, being several million miles nearer to the sun than Mars is, must have an appreciably shorter period of revolution. When it is in conjunction with Mars, or nearly so, as it is at present, the distance between the two is not very great, whereas when it is in the opposite part of its orbit they are separated by an enormous gap of space and the sun is between them."

"Manifestly in the latter case it would be perilous if not entirely impossible for the Martians to visit the golden asteroid, but when it is near Mars, as it is at present, and as it must be periodically for several years at a time, then is their opportunity."

"With their projectile cars sent forth with the aid of the mysterious explosives which they possess, it is easy for them under such circumstances, to make visits to the asteroid."

"Having obtained all the gold they need, or all that they can carry, a comparatively slight impulse given to their car, the direction of which is carefully calculated, will carry them back again to Mars."

"If that's so," exclaimed a voice, "we had better look out for ourselves! We have got into a very hornet's nest! If this is the place where the Martians come to dig gold, and if this is the height of their season, as you say, they are not likely to leave us here long undisturbed."

"These fellows must have been pirates that they had the fight with," said another.

"But what's become of the regulars, then?"

"Gone back to Mars for help, probably, and they'll be here again pretty quick, I am afraid!"

Considerable alarm was caused by this view of the case, and orders were sent to several of the electrical ships to cruise out to a safe distance in the direction of Mars and keep a sharp outlook for the approach of enemies.

Discovery That the Asteroid is a Solid Mass of Gold.

Meanwhile our prisoner awoke. He turned his eyes upon those standing about him, without any appearance of fear, but rather with a look of contempt, like that which Gulliver must have felt for the Lilliputians who had bound him under similar circumstances.

There were both hatred and defiance in his glance. He attempted to free himself, and the ropes strained with the tremendous pressure that he put upon them, but he could not break loose.

The Martian Safely Bound.

Satisfied that the Martian was safely bound, we left him where he lay, and, while awaiting news from the ships which had been sent to reconnoitre, continued the exploration of the little planet.

At a point nearly opposite to that where we had landed we came upon the mine which the Martians had been working. They had removed the thin coating of soil, laying bare the rich stores of gold beneath, and large quantities of the latter had been removed. Some of it was so solidly packed that the strokes of the instruments by means of which they had detached it were visible like the streaks left by a knife cutting cheese.

Reason for Astonishment.

The more we saw of this golden planet the greater became our astonishment. What the Martians had removed was a mere nothing in comparison with the entire bulk of the asteroid. Had the celestial mine been easier to reach, perhaps they would have removed more, or, possibly, their political economists perfectly understood the necessity of properly controlling the amount of precious metal in circulation. Very likely, we thought, the mining operations were under government control in Mars and it might be that the majority of the people there knew nothing of this store of wealth floating in the firmament. That would account for the battle with the supposed pirates, who, no doubt, had organized a secret expedition to the asteroid and been caught red-handed at the mine.

Richer Than the Klondike.

There were many detached masses of gold scattered about, and some of the men, on picking them up, exclaimed with astonishment at their lack of weight, forgetting for the moment that the same law which caused their own bodies to weigh so little must necessarily affect everything else in like degree.

A mass of gold that on the earth no man would have been able to lift could here be tossed about like a hollow rubber ball.

While we were examining the mine, one of the men left to guard the Martian came running to inform us that the latter evidently wished to make some communication. Mr. Edison and others hurried to the side of the prisoner. He still lay on his back, from which position he was not able to move, notwithstanding all his efforts. But by the motion of his eyes, aided by a pantomime with his fingers, he made us understand that there was something in a metallic box fastened at his side which he wished to reach.

The Martian's Treasure Box.

With some difficulty we succeeded in opening the box and in it there appeared a number of bright red pellets, as large as an ordinary egg.

When the Martian saw these in our hands he gave us to understand by the motion of his lips that he wished to swallow one of them. A pellet was accordingly placed in his mouth, and he instantly and with great eagerness swallowed it.

The Mysterious Pellets.

While trying to communicate his wishes to us, the prisoner had seemed to be in no little distress. He exhibited spasmodic movements which led some of the bystanders to think that he was on the point of dying, but within a few seconds after he had swallowed the pellet he appeared to be completely restored. All evidences of distress vanished, and a look of content came over his ugly face.

"It must be a powerful medicine," said one of the bystanders. "I wonder what it is."

"I will explain to you my notion," said Professor Moissan, the great French chemist. "I think it was a pill of the air, which he has taken."

"What do you mean by that?"

Artificial Atmosphere.

"My meaning is," said Professor Moissan, "that the Martian must have, for that he may live, the nitrogen and the oxygen. These can he not obtain here, where there is not the atmosphere. Therefore must he get them in some other manner. This has he managed to do by combining in these pills the oxygen and the nitrogen in the proportions which make atmospheric air. Doubtless upon Mars there are the very great chemists. They have discovered how this may be done. When the Martian has swallowed his little pill, the oxygen and the nitrogen are rendered to his blood as if he had breathed them, and so he can live with that air which has been distributed to him with the aid of his stomach in the place of his lungs."

If Monsieur Moissan's explanation was not correct, at any rate it seemed the only one that would fit the facts before us. Certainly the Martian could not breathe where there was practically no air, yet just as certainly after he had swallowed his pill he seemed as comfortable as any of us.

Signals from a Ship.

Suddenly, while we were gathered around the prisoner, and interested in this fresh evidence of the wonderful ingenuity of the Martians, and of their control over the processes of nature, one of the electrical ships that had been sent off in the direction of Mars was seen rapidly returning and displaying signals.

The Martians Are Coming.

It reported that the Martians were coming!

Chapter VIII

The alarm was spread instantly among those upon the planet and through the remainder of the fleet.

One of the men from the returning electrical ship dropped down upon the asteroid and gave a more detailed account of what they had seen.

His ship had been the one which had gone to the greatest distance in the direction of Mars. While cruising there, with all eyes intent, they had suddenly perceived a glittering object moving from the direction of the ruddy planet, and manifestly approaching them. A little inspection with the telescope had shown that it was one of the projectile cars used by the Martians.

Our ship had ventured so far from the asteroid that for a moment it seemed doubtful whether it would be able to return in time to give warning, because the electrical influence of the asteroid was comparatively slight at such a distance, and, after they had reversed their polarity, and applied their intensifier, so as to make that influence effective, their motion was at first exceedingly slow.

Fortunately after a time they got under way with sufficient velocity to bring them back to us before the approaching Martians could overtake them.

The latter were not moving with great velocity, having evidently projected themselves from Mars with only just sufficient force to throw them within the feeble sphere of gravitation of the asteroid, so that they should very gently land upon its surface.

Indeed, looking out behind the electrical ship which had brought us the warning, we immediately saw the projectile of the Martians approaching. It sparkled like a star in the black sky as the sunlight fell upon it.

Ready for the Enemy.

The ships of the squadron whose crews had not landed upon the planet were signalled to prepare for action, while those who were upon the asteroid made ready for battle there. A number of disintegrators were trained upon the approaching Martians, but Mr. Edison gave strict orders that no attempt should be made to discharge the vibratory force at random.

"They do not know that we are here," he said, "and I am convinced that they are unable to control their motions as we can do with our electrical ships. They depend simply upon the force of gravitation. Having passed the limit of the attraction of Mars, they have now fallen within the attraction of the asteroid, and they must slowly sink to its surface."

The Martians Cannot Stop.

"Having, as I am convinced, no means of producing or controlling electrical attraction and repulsion, they cannot stop themselves, but must come down upon the asteroid. Having got here they could never get away again, except as we know the survivors got away from earth, by propelling their projectile against gravitation with the aid of an explosive."

"Therefore, to a certain extent they will be at our mercy. Let us allow them quietly to land upon the planet, and then I think, if it becomes necessary, we can master them."

Notwithstanding Mr. Edison's reassuring words and manner, the company upon the asteroid experienced a dreadful suspense while the projectile which seemed very formidable as it drew near, sank with a slow and graceful motion toward the surface of the ground. Evidently it was about to land very near the spot where we stood awaiting it.

Its inmates had apparently just caught sight of us. They evinced signs of astonishment, and seemed at a loss exactly what to do. We could see projecting from the fore part of their car at least two of the polished knobs, whose fearful use and power we well comprehended.

Several of our men cried out to Mr. Edison in an extremity of terror:

"Why do you not destroy them? Be quick, or we shall all perish."

"No," said Mr. Edison, "there is no danger. You can see that they are not prepared. They will not attempt to attack us until they have made their landing."

The Martians Land.

And Mr. Edison was right. With gradually accelerated velocity, and yet very, very slowly in comparison with the speed they would have exhibited in falling upon such a planet as the earth, the Martians and their car came down to the ground.

We stood at a distance of perhaps three hundred feet from the point where they touched the asteroid. Instantly a dozen of the giants sprang from the car and gazed about for a moment with a look of intense surprise. At first it was doubtful whether they meant to attack us at all.

We stood on our guard, several carrying disintegrators in our hands, while a score more of these terrible engines were turned upon the Martians from the electrical ships which hovered near.

A Speech from Their Leader.

Suddenly he who seemed to be the leader of the Martians began to speak to them in pantomime, using his fingers after the manner in which they are used for conversation by deaf and dumb people.

Of course, we did not know what he was saying, but his meaning became perfectly evident a minute later. Clearly they did not comprehend the powers of the insignificant-looking strangers with whom they had to deal. Instead of turning their destructive engines upon us, they advanced on a run, with the evident purpose of making us prisoners or crushing us by main force.

Awed by the Disintegrator.

The soft whirr of the disintegrator in the hands of Mr. Edison standing near me came to my ears through the telephonic wire. He quickly swept the concentrating mirror a little up and down, and instantly the foremost Martian vanished! Part of some metallic dress that he wore fell upon the ground where he had stood, its vibratory rate not having been included in the range imparted to the disintegrator.

His followers paused for a moment, amazed, stared about as if looking for their leader, and then hurried back to their projectile and disappeared within it.

Mr. Edison Gives the Martians a Lesson.

The Martians could not comprehend the force of our destructive disintegrator. Its soft whirr in the hands of Mr. Edison came to my ears. Instantly the foremost Martian vanished! His followers paused for a moment, amazed, stared about looking for their leader, and then hurried back to their projectile and disappeared within it.

"Now we've got business on our hands," said Mr. Edison. "Look out for yourselves."

As he spoke, I saw the death-dealing knob of the war engine contained in the car of the Martians moving around toward us. In another instant it would have launched its destroying bolt.

Before that could occur, however, it had been dissipated into space by a vibratory stream from a disintegrator.

But we were not to get the victory quite so easily. There was another of the war engines in the car, and before we could concentrate our fire upon it, its awful flash shot forth, and a dozen of our comrades perished before our eyes.

"Quick! Quick!" shouted Mr. Edison to one of his electrical experts standing near. "There is something the matter with this disintegrator, and I cannot make it work. Aim at the knob, and don't miss it."

Martians and Terrestrians Fight a Terrible Battle.

But the aim was not well taken, and the vibratory force fell upon a portion of the car at a considerable distance from the knob, making a great breach, but leaving the engine uninjured.

A section of the side of the car had been destroyed, and the vibratory energy had spread no further. To have attempted to sweep the car from end to end would have been futile, because the period of action of the disintegrators during each discharge did not exceed one second, and distributing the energy over so great a space would have seriously weakened its power to shatter apart the atoms of the resisting substance. The disintegrators were like firearms, in that after each discharge they must be readjusted before they could be used again.

The Martians Are Desperate.

Through the breach we saw the Martians inside making desperate efforts to train their engine upon us, for after their first disastrous stroke we had rapidly shifted our position. Swiftly the polished knob, which gleamed like an evil eye, moved round to sweep over us. Instinctively, though incautiously, we had collected in a group.

A single discharge would sweep us all into eternity.

A Ticklish Position.

"Will no one fire upon them?" exclaimed Mr. Edison, struggling with the disintegrator in his hands, which still refused to work.

At this fearful moment I glanced around upon our company, and was astonished at the spectacle. In the presence of the danger many of them had lost all self-command. A half dozen had dropped their disintegrators upon the ground. Others stood as if frozen fast in their tracks. The expert electrician, whose poor aim had had such disastrous results, held in his hand an instrument which was in perfect condition, yet with mouth agape, he stood trembling like a captured bird.

The Electricians Lose Their Heads.

It was a disgraceful exhibition. Mr. Edison, however, had not lost his head. Again and again he sighted at the dreadful knob with his disintegrator, but the vibratory force refused to respond.

The means of safety were in our hands, and yet through a combination of ill luck and paralyzing terror we seemed unable to use them.

In a second more it would be all over with us.

The suspense in reality lasted only during the twinkling of an eye, though it seemed ages long.

Unable to endure it, I sharply struck the shoulder of the paralyzed electrician. To have attempted to seize the disintegrator from his hands would have been a fatal waste of time. Luckily the blow either roused him from his stupor or caused an instinctive movement of his hand that set the little engine in operation.

I am sure he took no aim, but providentially the vibratory force fell upon the desired point, and the knob disappeared.

Saved!

We were saved!

Instantly half a dozen rushed toward the car of the Martians. We bitterly repented their haste; they did not live to repent.

Unknown to us the Martians carried hand engines, capable of launching bolts of death of the same character as those which emanated from the knobs of their larger machines. With these they fired, so to speak, through the breach in their car, and four of our men who were rushing upon them fell in heaps of cinders. The effect of the terrible fire was like that which the most powerful strokes of lightning occasionally produce on earth.

The destruction of the threatening knob had instantaneously relieved the pressure upon the terror-stricken nerves of our company, and they had all regained their composure and self-command. But this new and unexpected disaster, following so close upon the fear which had recently overpowered them, produced a second panic, the effect of which was not to stiffen them in their tracks as before, but to send them scurrying in every direction in search of hiding places.

A Curious Effect.

And now a most curious effect of the smallness of the planet we were on began to play a conspicuous part in our adventures. Standing on a globe only five miles in diameter was like being on the summit of a mountain whose sides sloped rapidly off in every direction, disappearing in the black sky on all sides, as if it were some stupendous peak rising out of an unfathomable abyss.

In consequence of the quick rounding off of the sides of this globe, the line of the horizon was close at hand, and by running a distance of less than 250 yards the fugitives disappeared down the sides of the asteroid, and behind the horizon, even from the elevation of about fifteen feet from which the Martians were able to watch them. From our sight they disappeared much sooner.

The slight attraction of the planet and their consequent almost entire lack of weight enabled the men to run with immense speed. The result, as I subsequently learned, was that after they had disappeared from our view they quitted the planet entirely, the force being sufficient to partially free them from its gravitation, so that they sailed out into space, whirling helplessly end over end, until the elliptical orbits in which they travelled eventually brought them back again to the planet on the side nearly opposite to that from which they had departed.

Hunting for the Enemy.

But several of us, with Mr. Edison, stood fast, watching for an opportunity to get the Martians within range of the disintegrators. Luckily we were enabled, by shifting our position a little to the left, to get out of the line of sight of our enemies concealed in the car.

"If we cannot catch sight of them," said Mr. Edison, "we shall have to riddle the car on the chance of hitting them."

"It will be like firing into a bush to kill a hidden bear," said one of the party.

But help came from a quarter which was unexpected to us, although it should not have been so. Several of the electric ships had been hovering above us during the fight, their commanders being apparently uncertain how to act—fearful, perhaps, of injuring us in the attempt to smite our enemy.

But now the situation apparently lightened for them. They saw that we were at an immense disadvantage, and several of them immediately turned their batteries upon the car of the Martians.

They riddled it far more quickly and effectively than we could have done. Every stroke of the vibratory emanation made a gap in the side of the car, and we could perceive from the commotion within that our enemies were being rapidly massacred in their fortification.

The Electric Fleet's Disintegrating Batteries.

The batteries from the ships riddled the Martians' engine. Every stroke made a gap in the car, and our enemies were being rapidly massacred.

So overwhelming was the force and the advantage of the ships that in a little while it was all over. Mr. Edison signalled them to stop firing because it was plain that all resistance had ceased and probably not one of the Martians remained alive.

We now approached the car, which had been transpierced in every direction, and whose remaining portions were glowing with heat in consequence of the spreading of the atomic vibrations.

Immediately we discovered that all our anticipations were correct and that all of our enemies had perished.

The effect of the disintegrators upon them had been awful—too repulsive, indeed, to be described in detail. Some of the bodies had evidently entirely vanished; only certain metal articles which they had worn remaining, as in the case of the first Martian killed, to indicate that such beings had ever existed. The nature of the metal composing these articles was unknown to us. Evidently its vibratory rhythm did not correspond with any included in the ordinary range of the disintegrators.

The Disintegrators' Awful Effect.

Some of the giants had been only partially destroyed, the vibratory current having grazed them, in such a manner that the shattering undulations had not acted upon the entire body.

One thing that lends a peculiar horror to a terrestrial battlefield was absent; there was no bloodshed. The vibratory energy, not only completely destroyed whatever it fell upon but it seared the veins and arteries of the dismembered bodies so that there was no sanguinary exhibition connected with its murderous work.

All this time the shackled Martian had lain on his back where we had left him bound. What his feeling must have been may be imagined. At times, I caught a glimpse of his eyes, wildly rolling and exhibiting, when he saw that the victory was in our hands, the first indications of fear and terror shaking his soul that had yet appeared.

"That fellow is afraid at last," I said to Mr. Edison.

"Well, I should think he ought to be afraid," was the reply.

"So he ought, but if I am not mistaken this fear of his may be the beginning of a new discovery for us."

"How so?" asked Mr. Edison.

"In this way. When once he fears our power, and perceives that there would be no hope of contending against us, even if he were at liberty, he will respect us. This change in his mental attitude may tend to make him communicative. I do not see why we should despair of learning his language from him, and having done that, he will serve as our guide and interpreter, and will be of incalculable advantage to us when we have arrived at Mars."

"Capital! Capital!" said Mr. Edison. "We must concentrate the linguistic genius of our company upon that problem at once."

The Deserter's Return.

In the meantime some of the skulkers whose flight I have referred to began to return, chapfallen, but rejoicing in the disappearance of the danger. Several of them, I am ashamed to say, had been army officers. Yet possibly some excuse could be made for the terror by which they had been overcome. No man has a right to hold his fellow beings to account for the line of conduct they may pursue under circumstances which are not only entirely unexampled in their experience, but almost beyond the power of the imagination to picture.

Paralyzing terror had evidently seized them with the sudden comprehension of the unprecedented singularity of their situation. Millions of miles away from the earth, confronted on an asteroid by these diabolical monsters from a maleficent planet, who were on the point of destroying them with a strange torment of death—perhaps it was really more than human nature, deprived of the support of human surroundings, could have been expected to bear.

Those who, as already described, had run with so great a speed that they were projected, all unwilling, into space, rising in elliptical orbits from the surface of the planet, describing great curves in what might be denominated its sky, and then coming back again to the little globe on another side, were so filled with the wonders of their remarkable adventure that they had almost forgotten the terror which had inspired it.

There was nothing surprising in what had occurred to them the moment one considered the laws of gravitation on the asteroid, but their stories aroused an intense interest among all who listened to them.

Lord Kelvin was particularly interested, and while Mr. Edison was hastening preparations to quit the asteroid and resume our voyage to Mars, Lord Kelvin and a number of other scientific men instituted a series of remarkable experiments.

Jumping Into Empty Space.

It was one of the most laughable things imaginable to see Lord Kelvin, dressed in his air-tight suit, making tremendous jumps into empty space. It reminded me forcibly of what Lord Kelvin, then plain William Thompson, and Professor Blackburn had done when spending a Summer vacation at the seaside, while they were undergraduates of Cambridge University. They had spent all their time, to the surprise of onlookers, in spinning rounded stones on the beach, their object being to obtain a practical solution of the mathematical problem of "precession."

Lord Kelvin's Great Jump.

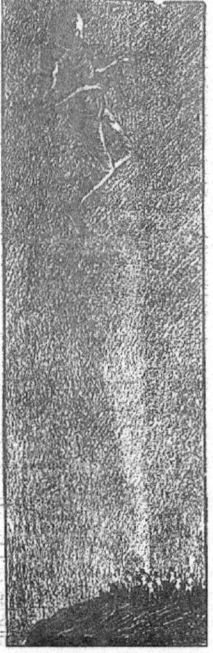

It was one of the most laughable things imaginable to see Lord Kelvin making tremendous jumps into empty space.

Immediately Lord Kelvin was imitated by a dozen others. With what seemed very slight effort they projected themselves straight upward, rising to a height of four hundred feet or more, and then slowly settling back again to the surface of the asteroid. The time of rise and fall combined was between three and four minutes.

On this little planet the acceleration of gravity or the velocity acquired by a falling body in one second was only four-fifths of an inch. A body required an entire minute to fall a distance of only 120 feet. Consequently, it was more like gradually settling than falling. The figures of these men of science, rising and sinking in this manner, appeared like so many gigantic marionettes bobbing up and down in a pneumatic bottle.

"Let us try that," said Mr. Edison, very much interested in the experiments.

A Delightful Experience.

Both of us jumped together. At first, with great swiftness, but gradually losing speed, we rose to an immense height straight from the ground. When we had reached the utmost limit of our flight we seemed to come to rest for a moment, and then began slowly, but with accelerated velocity, to sink back again to the planet. It was not only a peculiar but a delicious sensation, and but for strict orders which were issued that the electrical ships should be immediately prepared for departure, our entire company might have remained for an indefinite period enjoying this new kind of athletic exercise in a world where gravitation had become so humble that it could be trifled with.

While the final preparations for departure were being made, Lord Kelvin instituted other experiments that were no less unique in their results. The experience of those who had taken unpremeditated flights in elliptical orbits when they had run from the vicinity of the Martians suggested the throwing of solid objects in various directions from the surface of the planet in order to determine the distance that they would go and the curves they would describe in returning.

Mars, the Death-Dealing Planet, at Length at Hand!

For these experiments there was nothing more convenient or abundant than chunks of gold from the Martians' mine. These, accordingly, were hurled in various directions, and with every degree of velocity. A little calculation had shown that an initial velocity of thirty feet per second imparted to one of these chunks, moving at right angles to the radius of the asteroid, would, if the resistance of an almost inappreciable atmosphere were neglected, suffice to turn the piece of gold into a little satellite that would describe an orbit around the asteroid, and continue to do so forever, or at least until the slight atmospheric resistance should eventually bring it down to the surface.

But a less velocity than thirty feet per second would cause the golden missile to fly only part way around, while a greater velocity would give it an elliptical instead of a circular orbit, and in this ellipse it would continue to revolve around the asteroid in the character of a satellite.

If the direction of the original impulse were at more than a right angle to the radius of the asteroid, then the flying body would pass out to a greater or less distance in space in an elliptical orbit, eventually coming back again and falling upon the asteroid, but not at the same spot from which it had departed.

Interesting Experiments.

So many took part in these singular experiments, which assumed rather the appearance of outdoor sports than of scientific demonstrations, that in a short time we had provided the asteroid with a very large number of little moons, or satellites, of gold, which revolved around it in orbits of various degrees of ellipticity, taking, on the average, about three-quarters of an hour to complete a circuit. Since, on completing a revolution, they must necessarily pass through the point from which they started, they kept us constantly on the qui vive to avoid being knocked over by them as they swept around in their orbits.

Finally the signal was given for all to embark, and with great regret the savants quitted their scientific games and prepared to return to the electric ships.

Just on the moment of departure, the fact was announced by one, who had been making a little calculation on a bit of paper, that the velocity with which a body must be thrown in order to escape forever the attraction of the asteroid, and to pass on to an infinite distance in any direction, was only about forty-two feet in a second.

Manifestly it would be quite easy to impart such a speed as that to the chunks of gold that we held in our hands.

A Message to the Earth.

"Hurrah!" exclaimed one. "Let's send some of this back to the earth."

"Where is the earth?" asked another.

Being appealed to, several astronomers turned their eyes in the direction of the sun, where the black firmament was ablaze with stars, and in a moment recognized the earth-star shining there, with the moon attending close at hand.

"There," said one, "is the earth. Can you throw straight enough to hit it?"

"We'll try," was the reply, and immediately several threw huge golden nuggets in the direction of our far-away world, endeavoring to impart to them at least the required velocity of forty-two feet in a second, which would insure their passing beyond the attraction of the asteroid, and if there should be no disturbance on the way, and the aim were accurate, their eventual arrival upon the earth.

"Here's for you, Old Earth," said one of the throwers, "good luck, and more gold to you!"

If these precious missiles ever reached the earth we knew that they would plunge into the atmosphere like meteors and that probably the heat developed by their passage would melt and dissipate them in golden vapors before they could touch the ground.

Yet, there was a chance that some of them—if the aim were true—might survive the fiery passage through the atmosphere and fall upon the surface of our planet where, perhaps, they would afterward be picked up by a prospector and lead him to believe that he had struck a new bonanza.

But until we returned to the earth it would be impossible for us to tell what had become of the golden gifts which we had launched into space for our mother planet.

Chapter IX

All Aboard for Mars!

"All aboard!" was the signal, and the squadron having assembled under the lead of the flagship, we started again for Mars.

This time, as it proved, there was to be no further interruption, and when next we paused it was in the presence of the world inhabited by our enemies, and facing their frowning batteries.

Difficulty in Starting.

We did not find it so easy to start from the asteroid as it had been to start from the earth; that is to say, we could not so readily generate a very high velocity.

In consequence of the comparatively small size of the asteroid, its electric influence was very much less than that of the earth, and notwithstanding the appliances which we possessed for intensifying the electrical effect, it was not possible to produce a sufficient repulsion to start us off for Mars with anything like the impulse which we had received from the earth on our original departure.

The utmost velocity that we could generate did not exceed three miles in a second, and to get this required our utmost efforts. In fact, it had not seemed possible that we should attain even so great a speed as that. It was far more than we could have expected, and even Mr. Edison was surprised, as well as greatly gratified, when he found that we were moving with the velocity that I have named.

Mars 6,000,000 Miles Away.

We were still about 6,000,000 miles from Mars, so that, travelling three miles in a second, we should require at least twenty-three days to reach the immediate neighborhood of the planet.

Meanwhile we had a plenty of occupation to make the time pass quickly. Our prisoner was transported along with us, and we now began our attempts to ascertain what his language was, and, if possible, to master it ourselves.

Before quitting the asteroid we had found that it was necessary for him to swallow one of his "air pills," as Prof. Moissan called them, at least three times in the course of every twenty-four hours. One of us supplied him regularly and I thought that I could detect evidences of a certain degree of gratitude in his expression. This was encouraging, because it gave additional promise of the possibility of our being able to communicate with him in some more effective way than by mere signs. But once inside the car, where we had a supply of air kept at the ordinary pressure experienced on the earth, he could breathe like the rest of us.

Learning the Martians' Language.

The best linguists in the expedition, as Mr. Edison had suggested, were now assembled in the flagship, where the prisoner was, and they set to work to devise some means of ascertaining the manner in which he was accustomed to express his thoughts.

We had not heard him speak, because until we carried him into our car there was no atmosphere capable of conveying any sounds he might attempt to utter.

It seemed a fair assumption that the language of the Martians would be scientific in its structure. We had so much evidence of the practical bent of their minds, and of the immense progress which they had made in the direction of the scientific conquest of nature, that it was not to be supposed their medium of communication with one another would be lacking in clearness, or would possess any of the puzzling and unnecessary ambiguities that characterized the languages spoken on the earth.

"We shall not find them making he's and she's of stones, sticks and other inanimate objects," said one of the American linguists. "They must certainly have gotten rid of all that nonsense long ago."

"Ah," said a French professor from the Sorbonne, one of the makers of the never-to-be-finished dictionary. "It will be like the language of my country. Transparent, similar to the diamond, and sparkling as is the fountain."

The Volapuk of Mars.

"I think," said a German enthusiast, "that it will be a universal language, the Volapuk of Mars, spoken by all the inhabitants of that planet."

"But all these speculations," broke in Mr. Edison, "do not help you much. Why not begin in a practical manner by finding out what the Martian calls himself, for instance."

This seemed a good suggestion, and accordingly several of the bystanders began an expressive pantomime, intended to indicate to the giant, who was following all their motions with his eyes, that they wished to know by what name he called himself. Pointing their fingers to their own breasts they repeated, one after the other, the word "man."

If our prisoner had been a stupid savage, of course any such attempt as this to make him understand would have been idle. But it must be remembered that we were dealing with a personage who had presumably inherited from hundreds of generations the results of a civilization, and an intellectual advance, measured by the constant progress of millions of years.

Accordingly we were not very much astonished, when, after a few repetitions of the experiment, the Martian—one of whose arms had been partially released from its bonds in order to give him a little freedom of motion—imitated the action of his interrogators by pressing his finger over his heart.

The Martian Speaks.

Then, opening his mouth, he gave utterance to a sound which shook the air of the car like the hoarse roar of a lion. He seemed himself surprised by the noise he made, for he had not been used to speak in so dense an atmosphere.

Our ears were deafened and confused, and we recoiled in astonishment, not to say, half in terror.

With an ugly grin distorting his face as if he enjoyed our discomfiture, the Martian repeated the motion and the sound.

"R-r-r-r-r-h!"

It was not articulate to our ears, and not to be represented by any combination of letters.

"Faith," exclaimed a Dublin University professor, "if that's what they call themselves, how shall we ever translate their names when we come to write the history of the conquest?"

"Whist, mon," replied a professor from the University of Aberdeen, "let us whip the gillravaging villains first, and then we can describe than by any intitulation that may suit our deesposition."

The beginning of our linguistic conquest was certainly not promising, at least if measured by our acquirement of words, but from another point of view it was very gratifying, inasmuch as it was plain that the Martian understood what we were trying to do, and was, for the present, at least, disposed to aid us.

These efforts to learn the language of Mars were renewed and repeated every few hours, all the experience, learning and genius of the squadron being concentrated upon the work, and the result was that in the course of a few days we had actually succeeded in learning a dozen or more of the Martian's words and were able to make him understand us when we pronounced them, as well as to understand him when our ears had become accustomed to the growling of his voice.

Finally, one day the prisoner, who seemed to be in an unusually cheerful frame of mind, indicated that he carried in his breast some object which he wished us to see.

The Martian's Book.

With our assistance he pulled out a book!

Actually, it was a book, not very unlike the books which we have upon the earth, but printed, of course, in characters that were entirely strange and unknown to us. Yet these characters evidently gave expression to a highly intellectual language. All those who were standing by at the moment uttered a shout of wonder and of delight, and the cry of "A book! a book!" ran around the circle, and the good news was even promptly communicated to some of the neighboring electric ships of the squadron. Several other learned men were summoned in haste from them to examine our new treasure.

How the Earth Men Learned the Martian Language.

Actually, it was a book that the prisoner produced, and then he proceeded to teach us, as well as he could, several words of his language.

The Martian, whose good nature had manifestly been growing day after day, watched our inspection of his book with evidences of great interest, not unmingled with amusement. Finally he beckoned the holder of the book to his side, and placing his broad finger upon one of the huge letters—if letters they were, for they more nearly resembled the characters employed by the Chinese printer—he uttered a sound which we, of course, took to be a word, but which was different from any we had yet heard. Then he pointed to one after another of us standing around.

"Ah," explained everybody, the truth being apparent, "that is the word by which the Martians designate us. They have a name, then, for the inhabitants of the earth."

"Or, perhaps, it is rather the name for the earth itself," said one.

But this could not, of course, be at once determined. Anyhow, the word, whatever its precise meaning might be, had now been added to our vocabulary, although as yet our organs of speech proved unable to reproduce it in a recognizable form.

This promising and unexpected discovery of the Martian's book lent added enthusiasm to those who were engaged in the work of trying to master the language of our prisoner, and the progress that they made in the course of the next few days was truly astonishing. If the prisoner had been unwilling to aid them, of course, it would have been impossible to proceed, but, fortunately for us, he seemed more and more to enter into the spirit of the undertaking, and actually to enjoy it himself. So bright and quick was his understanding that he was even able to indicate to us methods of mastering his language that would otherwise, probably, never have occurred to our minds.

The Prisoner Teaches.

In fact, in a very short time he had turned teacher and all these learned men, pressing around him with eager attention, had become his pupils.

I cannot undertake to say precisely how much of the Martian language had been acquired by the chief linguists of the expedition before the time when we arrived so near to Mars that it became necessary for most of us to abandon our studies in order to make ready for the more serious business which now confronted us.

But, at any rate, the acquisition was so considerable as to allow of the interchange of ordinary ideas with our prisoner, and there was no longer any doubt that he would be able to give us much information when we landed on his native planet.

At the end of twenty-three days as measured by terrestrial time, since our departure from the asteroid, we arrived in the sky of Mars.

For a long time the ruddy planet had been growing larger and more formidable, gradually turning from a huge star into a great red moon, and then expanding more and more until it began to shut out from sight the constellations behind it. The curious markings on its surface, which from the earth can only be dimly glimpsed with a powerful telescope, began to reveal themselves clearly to our naked eyes.

I have related how even before we had reached the asteroid, Mars began to present a most imposing appearance as we saw it with our telescopes. Now, however, that it was close at hand, the naked eye view of the planet was more wonderful than anything we had been able to see with telescopes when at a greater distance.

Mars in Sight.

We were approaching the southern hemisphere of Mars in about latitude 45 degrees south. It was near the time of the vernal equinox in that hemisphere of the planet, and under the stimulating influence of the Spring sun, rising higher and higher every day, some such awakening of life and activity upon its surface as occurs on the earth under similar circumstances was evidently going on.

Around the South Pole were spread immense fields of snow and ice, gleaming with great brilliance. Cutting deep into the borders of these ice fields, we could see broad channels of open water, indicating the rapid breaking of the grip of the frost.

The First Close Sight of the Planet Which Nearly Conquered the Earth.

Around the South Pole were spread immense fields of snow and ice, gleaming with great brilliancy.

Almost directly beneath us was a broad oval region, light red in color, to which terrestrial astronomers had given the name of Hellas. Toward the south, between Hellas and the borders of the polar ice, was a great belt of darkness that astronomers had always been inclined to regard as a sea. Looking toward the north, we could perceive the immense red expanses of the continents of Mars, with the long curved line of the Syrtis Major, or "The Hour Glass Sea," sweeping through the midst of them toward the north until it disappeared under the horizon.

Crossing and recrossing the red continents, in every direction, were the canals of Schiaparelli.

Mars Reached at Last—Thrilling Adventures.

Plentifully sprinkled over the surface we could see brilliant points, some of dazzling brightness, outshining the daylight. There was also an astonishing variety in the colors of the broad expanses beneath us. Activity, vivacity and beauty, such as we were utterly unprepared to behold, expressed their presence on all sides.

The excitement on the flagship and among the other members of the squadron was immense. It was certainly a thrilling scene. Here, right under our feet, lay the world we had come to do battle with. Its appearances, while recalling in some of their broader aspects those which it had presented when viewed from our observatories, were far more strange, complex and wonderful than any astronomer had ever dreamed of. Suppose all of our anticipations about Mars should prove to have been wrong, after all?

There could be no longer any question that it was a world which, if not absolutely teeming with inhabitants, like a gigantic ant-hill, at any rate bore on every side the marks of their presence and of their incredible undertakings and achievements.

Here and there clouds of smoke arose and spread slowly through the atmosphere beneath us. Floating higher above the surface of the planet were clouds of vapor, assuming the familiar forms of stratus and cumulus with which we were acquainted upon the earth.

Dense Clouds Appear.

These clouds, however, seemed upon the whole to be much less dense than those to which we were accustomed at home. They had, too, a peculiar iridescent beauty as if there was something in their composition or their texture which split up the chromatic elements of the sunlight and thus produced internal rainbow effects that caused some of the heavier cloud masses to resemble immense collections of opals, alive with the play of ever-changing colors and magically suspended above the planet.

As we continued to study the phenomena that was gradually unfolded beneath us we thought that we could detect in many places evidences of the existence of strong fortifications. The planet of war appeared to be prepared for the attacks of enemies. Since, as our own experience had shown, it sometimes waged war with distant planets, it was but natural that it should be found prepared to resist foes who might be disposed to revenge themselves for injuries suffered at its hands.

The Wonderful Battlements of Mars.

Approaching the planet, the extraordinary fortifications of the Martians were plainly shown. It was an awe-inspiring spectacle and proved to us their superiority over our terrestrial defences.

As had been expected, our prisoner now proved to be of very great assistance to us. Apparently he took a certain pride in exhibiting to strangers from a distant world the beauties and wonders of his own planet.

The Martian Is Understood.

We could not understand by any means all that he said, but we could readily comprehend, from his gestures, and from the manner in which his features lighted up at the recognition of familiar scenes and objects, what his sentiments in regard to them were, and, in a general way, what part they played in the life of the planet.

He confirmed our opinion that certain of the works which we saw beneath us were fortifications, intended for the protection of the planet against invaders from outer space. A cunning and almost diabolical look came into his eyes as he pointed to one of these strongholds.

Cause for Anxiety.

His confidence and his mocking looks were not reassuring to us. He knew what his planet was capable of, and we did not. He had seen, on the asteroid, the extent of our power, and while its display served to intimidate him there, yet now that he and we together were facing the world of his birth, his fear had evidently fallen from him, and he had the manner of one who feels that the shield of an all-powerful protector had been extended over him.

But it could not be long now before we should ascertain, by the irrevocable test of actual experience, whether the Martians possessed the power to annihilate us or not.

How shall I describe our feelings as we gazed at the scene spread beneath us? They were not quite the same as those of the discoverer of new lands upon the earth. This was a whole new world that we had discovered, and it was filled, as we could see, with inhabitants.

But that was not all. We had not come with peaceful intentions.

We were to make war on this new world.

Deducting our losses we had not more than 940 men left. With these we were to undertake the conquest of a world containing we could not say how many millions!

A Hard Task Ahead.

Our enemies, instead of being below us in the scale of intelligence were, we had every reason to believe, greatly our superiors. They had proved that they possessed a command over the powers of nature such as we, up to the time when Mr. Edison made his inventions, had not even dreamed that it was possible for us to obtain.

It was true that at present we appeared to have the advantage, both in our electrical ships and in our means of offence. The disintegrator was at least as powerful an engine of destruction as any that the Martians had yet shown that they possessed. It did not seem that in that respect they could possibly excel us.

During the brief war with the Martians upon the earth it had been gunpowder against a mysterious force as much stronger than gunpowder as the latter was superior to the bows and arrows that preceded it.

There had been no comparison whatever between the offensive means employed by the two parties in the struggle on the earth.

But the genius of one man had suddenly put us on the level of our enemies in regard to fighting capacity.

Then, too, our electrical ships were far more effective for their purpose than the projectile cars used by the Martians. In fact, the principle upon which they were based was, at bottom, so simple that it seemed astonishing the Martians had not hit upon it.

Mr. Edison himself was never tired of saying in reference to this matter:

The Martians a Mystery.

"I cannot understand why the Martians did not invent these things. They have given ample proof that they understand electricity better than we do. Why should they have resorted to the comparatively awkward and bungling means of getting from one planet to another that they have employed when they might have ridden through the solar system in such conveyances as ours with perfect ease?"

"And besides," Mr. Edison would add, "I cannot understand why they did not employ the principle of harmonic vibrations in the construction of their engines of war. The lightning-like strokes that they deal from their machines are no doubt equally powerful, but I think the range of destruction covered by the disintegrators is greater."

However, these questions must remain open until we could effect a landing on Mars, and learn something of the condition of things there.

The thing that gave us the most uneasiness was the fact that we did not yet know what powers the Martians might have in reserve. It was but natural to suppose that here, on their own ground, they would possess means of defence even more effective than the offensive engines they had employed in attacking enemies so many millions of miles from home.

It was important that we should waste no time, and it was equally important that we should select the most vulnerable point for attack. It was self-evident, therefore, that our first duty would be to reconnoitre the surface of the planet and determine its weakest point of defence.

At first Mr. Edison contemplated sending the various ships in different directions around the planet in order that the work of exploration might be quickly accomplished. But upon second thought it seemed wiser to keep the squadron together, thus diminishing the chance of disaster.

Besides, the commander wished to see with his own eyes the exact situation of the various parts of the planet, where it might appear advisable for us to begin our assault.

Thus far we had remained suspended at so great a height above the planet that we had hardly entered into the perceptible limits of its atmosphere and there was no evidence that we had been seen by the inhabitants of Mars; but before starting on our voyage of exploration it was determined to drop down closer to the surface in order that we might the more certainly identify the localities over which we passed.

This manoeuvre nearly got us into serious trouble.

A Huge Airship.

When we had arrived within a distance of three miles from the surface of Mars we suddenly perceived approaching from the eastward a large airship which was navigating the Martian atmosphere at a height of perhaps half a mile above the ground.

The Martians in Their Airship.

When we arrived within a distance of three miles from the surface of Mars we suddenly perceived approaching from the eastward a large airship which was navigating the Martian atmosphere at a height of perhaps half a mile above the ground.

More Stirring Adventures of Our Warriors Against Mars.

This airship moved rapidly on to a point nearly beneath us, when it suddenly paused, reversed its course, and evidently made signals, the purpose of which was not at first evident to us.

But in a short time their meaning became perfectly plain, when we found ourselves surrounded by at least twenty similar aerostats approaching swiftly from different sides.

It was a great mystery to us where so many airships had been concealed previous to their sudden appearance in answer to the signals.

But the mystery was quickly solved when we saw detaching itself from the surface of the planet beneath us, where, while it remained immovable, its color had blended with that of the soil so as to render it invisible, another of the mysterious ships.

Then our startled eyes beheld on all sides these formidable-looking enemies rising from the ground beneath us like so many gigantic insects, disturbed by a sudden alarm.

In a short time the atmosphere a mile or two below us, and to a distance of perhaps twenty miles around in every direction, was alive with airships of various sizes, and some of most extraordinary forms, exchanging signals, rushing to and fro, but all finally concentrating beneath the place where our squadron was suspended.

We had poked the hornet's nest with a vengeance!

As yet there had been no sting, but we might quickly expect to feel it if we did not get out of range.

Escaping Danger.

Quickly instructions were flashed throughout the squadron to instantly reverse polarities and rise as swiftly as possible to a great height.

It was evident that this manoeuvre would save us from danger if it were quickly effected, because the airships of the Martians were simply airships and nothing more. They could only float in the atmosphere, and had no means of rising above it, or of navigating empty space.

To have turned our disintegrators upon them, and to have begun a battle then and there, would have been folly.

They overwhelmingly outnumbered us, the majority of them were yet at a considerable distance and we could not have done battle, even with our entire squadron acting together, with more than one-quarter of them simultaneously. In the meantime the others would have surrounded and might have destroyed us. We must first get some idea of the planet's means of defence before we ventured to assail it.

Having risen rapidly to a height of twenty-five or thirty miles, so that we could feel confident that our ships had vanished at least from the naked eye view of our enemies beneath, a brief consultation was held.

It was determined to adhere to our original programme and to circumnavigate Mars in every direction before proceeding to open the war.

Intimidated by the Enemy.

The overwhelming forces shown by the enemy had intimidated even some of the most courageous of our men, but still it was universally felt that it would not do to retreat without a blow struck.

The more we saw of the power of the Martians, the more we became convinced that there would be no hope for the earth, if these enemies ever again effected a landing upon its surface, the more especially since our squadron contained nearly all of the earth's force that would be effective in such a contest.

With Mr. Edison and the other men of science away, they would not be able at home to construct such engines as we possessed, or to manage them even if they were constructed.

Our planet had staked everything on a single throw.

These considerations again steeled our hearts, and made us bear up as bravely as possible in the face of the terrible odds that confronted us.

Turning the noses of our electrical ships toward the west, we began our circumnavigation.

Chapter X

At first we rose to a still greater height, in order more effectually to escape the watchful eyes of our enemies, and then, after having moved rapidly several hundred miles toward the west, we dropped down again within easy eyeshot of the surface of the planet, and commenced our inspection.

When we originally reached Mars, as I have related, it was at a point in its southern hemisphere, in latitude 45 degrees south, and longitude 75 degrees east, that we first closely approached its surface. Underneath us was the land called "Hellas," and it was over this land of Hellas that the Martian air fleet had suddenly made its appearance.

Our westward motion, while at a great height above the planet, had brought us over another oval-shaped land called "Noachia," surrounded by the dark ocean, the "Mare Erytraeum." Now approaching nearer the surface our course was changed so as to carry us toward the equator of Mars.

We passed over the curious, half-drowned continent known to terrestrial astronomers as the Region of Deucalion, then across another sea, or gulf, until we found ourselves floating, at a height of perhaps five miles, above a great continental land, at least three thousand miles broad from east to west, and which I immediately recognized as that to which astronomers had given the various names of "Aeria," "Edom," "Arabia," and "Eden."

Here the spectacle became of breathless interest.

"Wonderful! Wonderful!"

"Who could have believed it!"

Such were the exclamations heard on all sides.

When at first we were suspended above Hellas, looking toward the north, the northeast and the northwest, we had seen at a distance some of these great red regions, and had perceived the curious network of canals by which they were intersected. But that was a far-off and imperfect view.

Now, when we were near at hand and straight above one of these singular lands, the magnificence of the panorama surpassed belief.

From the earth about a dozen of the principal canals crossing the continent beneath us had been perceived, but we saw hundreds, nay, thousands of them!

It was a double system, intended both for irrigation and for protection, and far more marvellous in its completeness than the boldest speculative minds among our astronomers had ever dared to imagine.

"Ha! that's what I always said," exclaimed a veteran from one of our great observatories. "Mars is red because its soil and vegetation are red."

And certainly appearances indicated that he was right.

There were no green trees, and there was no green grass. Both were red, not of a uniform red tint, but presenting an immense variety of shades which produced a most brilliant effect, fairly dazzling our eyes.

But what trees! And what grass! And what flowers!

Gigantic Vegetation.

Our telescopes showed that even the smaller trees must be 200 or 300 feet in height, and there were forests of giants, whose average height was evidently at least 1,000 feet.

"That's all right," exclaimed the enthusiast I have just quoted. "I knew it would be so. The trees are big, for the same reason that the men are, because the planet is small, and they can grow big without becoming too heavy to stand."

Flashing in the sun on all sides were the roofs of metallic buildings, which were evidently the only kind of edifices that Mars possessed. At any rate, if stone or wood were employed in their construction both were completely covered with metallic plates.

This added immensely to the warlike aspect of the planet. For warlike it was. Everywhere we recognized fortified stations, glittering with an array of the polished knobs of the lightning machines, such as we had seen in the land of Hellas.

From the land of Edom, directly over the equator of the planet, we turned our faces westward, and, skirting the Mare Erytraeum, arrived above the place where the broad canal known as the Indus empties into the sea.

Before us, and stretching away toward the northwest, now lay the continent of Chryse, a vast red land, oval in outline, and surrounded and crossed by innumerable canals. Chryse was not less than 1,600 miles across, and it, too, evidently swarmed with giant inhabitants.

But the shadow of night lay upon the greater portion of the land of Chryse. In our rapid motion westward we had outstripped the sun and had now arrived at a point where day and night met upon the surface of the planet beneath us.

Behind all was brilliant with sunshine, but before us the face of Mars gradually disappeared in the deepening gloom. Through the darkness, far away, we could behold magnificent beams of electric light darting across the curtain of night, and evidently serving to illuminate towns and cities that lay beneath.

We pushed on into the night for two or three hundred miles over that part of the continent of Chryse whose inhabitants were doubtless enjoying the deep sleep that accompanies the dark hours immediately preceding the dawn. Still everywhere splendid clusters of light lay like fallen constellations upon the ground, indicating the sites of great towns, which, like those of the earth, never sleep.

But this scene, although weird and beautiful, could give us little of the kind of information we were in search of.

Accordingly it was resolved to turn back eastward until we had arrived in the twilight space separating day and night, and then hover over the planet at that point, allowing it to turn beneath us so that, as we looked down, we should see in succession the entire circuit of the globe of Mars while it rolled under our eyes.

The rotation of Mars on its axis is performed in a period very little longer than that of the earth's rotation, so that the length of the day and night in the world of Mars is only some forty minutes longer than their length upon the earth.

In thus remaining suspended over the planet, on the line of daybreak, so to speak, we believed that we should be peculiarly safe from detection by the eyes of the inhabitants. Even astronomers are not likely to be wide awake just at the peep of dawn. Almost all of the inhabitants, we confidently believed, would still be sound asleep upon that part of the planet passing directly beneath us, and those who were awake would not be likely to watch for unexpected appearances in the sky.

Besides, our height was so great that notwithstanding the numbers of the squadron, we could not easily be seen from the surface of the planet, and if seen at all we might be mistaken for high-flying birds.

Mars Passes Below Us.

Here we remained then through the entire course of twenty-four hours and saw in succession as they passed from night into day beneath our feet the land of Chryse, the great continent of Tharsis, the curious region of intersecting canals which puzzled astronomers on the earth had named the "Gordian Knot," the continental lands of Memnonia, Amazonia and Aeolia, the mysterious centre where hundreds of vast canals came together from every direction, called the Trivium Charontis; the vast circle of Elysium, a thousand miles across, and completely surrounded by a broad green canal; the continent of Libya, which, as I remembered, had been half covered by a tremendous inundation whose effects were visible from the earth in the year 1889, and finally the long, dark sea of the Syrtis Major, lying directly south of the land of Hellas.

The excitement and interest which we all experienced were so great that not one of us took a wink of sleep during the entire twenty-four hours of our marvellous watch.

There are one or two things of special interest amid the multitude of wonderful observations that we made which I must mention here on account of their connection with the important events that followed soon after.

Just west of the land of Chryse we saw the smaller land of Ophir, in the midst of which is a singular spot called the Juventae Fons, and this Fountain of Youth, as our astronomers, by a sort of prophetic inspiration, had named it, proved later to be one of the most incredible marvels on the planet Mars.

Further to the west, and north from the great continent of Tharsis, we beheld the immense oval-shaped land of Thaumasia containing in its centre the celebrated "Lake of the Sun," a circular body of water not less than 500 miles in diameter, with dozens of great canals running away from it like the spokes of a wheel in every direction, thus connecting it with the ocean which surrounds it on the south and east, and with the still larger canals that encircle it toward the north and west.

This Lake of the Sun came to play a great part in our subsequent adventures. It was evident to us from the beginning that it was the chief centre of population on the planet. It lies in latitude 25 degrees South and longitude about 90 degrees west.

Completing the Circuit.

Having completed the circuit of the Martian globe, we were moved by the same feeling which every discoverer of new lands experiences, and immediately returned to our original place above the land of Hellas, because since that was the first part of Mars that we had seen, we felt a greater degree of familiarity with it than with any other portion of the planet, and there, in a certain sense, we felt "at home."

But, as it proved, our enemies were on the watch for us there. We had almost forgotten them, so absorbed were we by the great spectacles that had been unrolling themselves beneath our feet.

We ought, of course, to have been a little more cautious in approaching the place where they first caught sight of us, since we might have known that they would remain on the watch near that spot.

But at any rate they had seen us, and it was now too late to think of taking them again by surprise.

They on their part had a surprise in store for us, which was greater than any we had yet experienced.

We saw their ships assembling once more far down in the atmosphere beneath us, and we thought we could detect evidences of something unusual going on upon the surface of the planet.

Suddenly from the ships, and from various points on the ground beneath, there rose high in the air, and carried by invisible currents in every direction, immense volumes of black smoke, or vapor, which blotted out of sight everything below them!

The All-Powerful War-Cloud of the Martians.

Suddenly from the ships there arose high in the air immense volumes of black smoke, which blotted out of sight everything below them!

South, north, west and east, the curtain of blackness rapidly spread, until the whole face of the planet as far as our eyes could reach, and the airships thronging under us, were all concealed from sight!

Mars had played the game of the cuttlefish, which, when pursued by its enemies, darkens the water behind it by a sudden outgush of inky fluid, and thus escapes the eye of its foe.

The Great Smoke Cloud.

Our Warriors Find the Martians to Be Foes Worth Fearing.

The eyes of man had never beheld such a spectacle!

Where a few minutes before the sunny face of a beautiful and populous planet had been shining beneath us, there was now to be seen nothing but black, billowing clouds, swelling up everywhere like the mouse-colored smoke that pours from a great transatlantic liner when fresh coal has just been heaped upon her fires.

In some places the smoke spouted upward in huge jets to the height of several miles; elsewhere it eddied in vast whirlpools of inky blackness.

Not a glimpse of the hidden world beneath was anywhere to be seen.

Mars Wears Its War Mask.

Mars had put on its war mask, and fearful indeed was the aspect of it!

After the first pause of surprise the squadron quickly backed away into the sky, rising rapidly, because, from one of the swirling eddies beneath us the smoke began suddenly to pile itself up in an enormous aerial mountain, whose peaks shot higher and higher, with apparently increasing velocity, until they seemed about to engulf us with their tumbling ebon masses.

Unaware what the nature of this mysterious smoke might be, and fearing it was something more than a shield for the planet, and might be destructive to life, we fled before it, as before the onward sweep of a pestilence.

Directly underneath the flagship, one of the aspiring smoke peaks grew with most portentous swiftness, and, notwithstanding all our efforts, in a little while it had enveloped us.

The Stifling Smoke.

Several of us were standing on the deck of the electrical ship. We were almost stifled by the smoke, and were compelled to take refuge within the car, where, until the electric lights had been turned on, darkness so black that it oppressed the strained eyeballs prevailed.

But in this brief experience, terrifying though it was, we had learned one thing. The smoke would kill by strangulation, but evidently there was nothing especially poisonous in its nature. This fact might be of use to us in our subsequent proceedings.

"This spoils our plans," said the commander. "There is no use of remaining here for the present; let us see how far this thing extends."

At first we rose straight away to a height of 200 or 300 miles, thus passing entirely beyond the sensible limits of the atmosphere, and far above the highest point that the smoke could reach.

From this commanding point of view our line of sight extended to an immense distance over the surface of Mars in all directions. Everywhere the same appearance; the whole planet was evidently covered with the smoke.

A Wonderful System.

A complete telegraphic system evidently connected all the strategic points upon Mars, so that, at a signal from the central station, the wonderful curtain could be instantaneously drawn over the entire face of the planet.

In order to make certain that no part of Mars remained uncovered, we dropped down again nearer to the upper level of the smoke clouds, and then completely circumnavigated the planet. It was thought possible that on the night side no smoke would be found and that it would be practicable for us to make a descent there.

But when we had arrived on that side of Mars which was turned away from the sun, we no longer saw beneath us, as we had done on our previous visit to the night hemisphere of the planet, brilliant groups and clusters of electric lights beneath us. All was dark.

In fact, so completely did the great shell of smoke conceal the planet that the place occupied by the latter seemed to be simply a vast black hole in the firmament.

The sun was hidden behind it, and so dense was the smoke that even the solar rays were unable to penetrate it, and consequently there was no atmospheric halo visible around the concealed planet.

All the sky around was filled with stars, but their countless host suddenly disappeared when our eyes turned in the direction of Mars. The great black globe blotted them out without being visible itself.

Attempts to Attack Baffled.

"Apparently we can do nothing here," said Mr. Edison. "Let us return to the daylight side."

When we had arrived near the point where we had been when the wonderful phenomenon first made its appearance, we paused, and then, at the suggestion of one of the chemists, dropped close to the surface of the smoke curtain which had now settled down into comparative quiescence, in order that we might examine it a little more critically.

The flagship was driven into the smoke cloud so deeply that for a minute we were again enveloped in night. A quantity of the smoke was entrapped in a glass jar.

Examining the Smoke.

Rising again into the sunlight, the chemists began an examination of the constitution of the smoke. They were unable to determine its precise character, but they found that its density was astonishingly slight. This accounted for the rapidity with which it had risen, and the great height which it had attained in the comparatively light atmosphere of Mars.

"It is evident," said one of the chemists, "that this smoke does not extend down to the surface of the planet. From what the astronomers say as to the density of the air on Mars, it is probable that a clear space of at least a mile in height exists between the surface of Mars and the lower limit of the smoke curtain. Just how deep the latter is we can only determine by experiment, but it would not be surprising if the thickness of this great blanket which Mars has thrown around itself should prove to be a quarter or half a mile."

"Anyhow," said one of the United States army officers, "they have dodged out of sight, and I don't see why we should not dodge in and get at them. If there is clear air under the smoke, as you think, why couldn't the ships dart down through the curtain and come to a close tackle with the Martians?"

"It would not do at all," said the commander. "We might simply run ourselves into an ambush. No; we must stay outside, and if possible fight them from here."

Strategic Measures Employed.

"They can't keep this thing up forever," said the officer. "Perhaps the smoke will clear off after a while, and then we will have a chance."

"Not much hope of that, I am afraid," said the chemist who had originally spoken. "This smoke could remain floating in the atmosphere for weeks, and the only wonder to me is how they ever expect to get rid of it, when they think their enemies have gone and they want some sunshine again."

"All that is mere speculation," said Mr. Edison; "let us get at something practical. We must do one of two things: either attack them shielded as they are, or wait until the smoke has cleared away. The only other alternative, that of plunging blindly down through the curtain, is at present not to be thought of."

"I am afraid we couldn't stand a very long siege ourselves," suddenly remarked the chief commissary of the expedition, who was one of the members of the flagship's company.

"What do you mean by that?" asked Mr. Edison sharply, turning to him.

"Well, sir, you see," said the commissary, stammering, "our provisions wouldn't hold out."

"Wouldn't hold out?" exclaimed Mr. Edison, in astonishment, "why, we have compressed and prepared provisions enough to last this squadron for three years."

"We had, sir, when we left the earth," said the commissary, in apparent distress, "but I am sorry to say that something has happened."

"Something has happened! Explain yourself!"

Accident to the Stores.

"I don't know what it is, but on inspecting some of the compressed stores, a short time ago, I found that a large number of them were destroyed, whether through leakage of air, or what, I am unable to say. I sent to inquire as to the condition of the stores in the other ships in the squadron and I found that a similar condition of things prevailed there."

"The fact is," continued the commissary, "we have only provisions enough, in proper condition, for about ten days' consumption."

"After that we shall have to forage on the country, then," said the army officer.

"Why did you not report this before?" demanded Mr. Edison.

"Because, sir," was the reply, "the discovery was not made until after we arrived close to Mars, and since then there has been so much excitement that I have hardly had time to make an investigation and find out what the precise condition of affairs is; besides, I thought we should land upon the planet and then we would be able to renew our supplies."

I closely watched Mr. Edison's expression in order to see how this most alarming news would affect him. Although he fully comprehended its fearful significance, he did not lose his self-command.

We Must Act Quickly.

"Well, well," he said, "then it will become necessary for us to act quickly. Evidently we cannot wait for the smoke to clear off, even if there were any hope of its clearing. We must get down on Mars now, having conquered it first if possible, but anyway we must get down there, in order to avoid starvation."

"It is very lucky," he continued, "that we have ten days' supply left. A great deal can be done in ten days."

A few hours after this the commander called me aside, and said:

"I have thought it all out. I am going to reconstruct some of our disintegrators, so as to increase their range and their power. Then I am going to have some of the astronomers of the expedition locate for me the most vulnerable points upon the planet, where the population is densest and a hard blow would have the most effect, and I am going to pound away at them, through the smoke, and see whether we cannot draw them out of their shell."

A Plan Arranged.

With his expert assistants Mr. Edison set to work at once to transform a number of the disintegrators into still more formidable engines of the same description. One of these new weapons having been distributed to each of the members of the squadron, the next problem was to decide where to strike.

When we first examined the surface of the planet it will be remembered that we had regarded the Lake of the Sun and its environs as being the very focus of the planet. While it might also be a strong point of defence, yet an effective blow struck there would go to the enemy's heart and be more likely to bring the Martians promptly to terms than anything else.

The first thing, then, was to locate the Lake of the Sun on the smoke-hidden surface of the planet beneath us. This was a problem that the astronomers could readily solve.

Fortunately, in the flagship itself there was one of the star-gazing gentlemen who had made a specialty of the study of Mars. That planet, as I have already explained, was now in opposition to the earth. The astronomer had records in his pocket which enabled him, by a brief calculation, to say just when the Lake of the Sun would be on the meridian of Mars as seen from the earth. Our chronometers still kept terrestrial time; we knew the exact number of days and hours that had elapsed since we had departed, and so it was possible by placing ourselves in a line between the earth and Mars to be practically in the situation of an astronomer in his observatory at home.

Then it was only necessary to wait for the hour when the Lake of the Sun would be upon the meridian of Mars in order to be certain what the true direction of the latter from the flagship was.

Having thus located the heart of our foe behind its shield of darkness, we prepared to strike.

The Smoke Must Be Shattered.

"I have ascertained," said Mr. Edison, "the vibration period of the smoke, so that it will be easy for us to shatter it into invisible atoms. You will see that every stroke of the disintegrators will open a hole through the black curtain. If their field of destruction could be made wide enough, we might in that manner clear away the entire covering of smoke, but all that we shall really be able to do will be to puncture it with holes, which will, perhaps, enable us to catch glimpses of the surface beneath. In that manner we may be able more effectually to concentrate our fire upon the most vulnerable points."

The Blow—And Its Effect.

Everything being prepared, and the entire squadron having assembled to watch the effect of the opening blow and be ready to follow it up, Mr. Edison himself poised one of the new disintegrators, which was too large to be carried in the hand, and, following the direction indicated by the calculations of the astronomers, launched the vibratory discharge into the ocean of blackness beneath.

A Terrible Encounter.

The Martians and Our Warriors Fight a Battle to the Death.

Instantly there opened beneath us a huge well-shaped hole, from which the black clouds rolled violently back in every direction.

Edison Triumphs Over the Martians' Device.

Instantly there opened beneath us a huge, well-shaped hole, from which the black clouds rolled back in every direction.

Through this opening we saw the gleam of brilliant lights beneath.

We had made a hit.

"It is the Lake of the Sun!" shouted the astronomer who furnished the calculation by means of which its position had been discovered.

And, indeed, it was the Lake of the Sun. While the opening in the clouds made by the discharge was not wide, yet it sufficed to give us a view of a portion of the curving shore of the lake, which was ablaze with electric lights.

Whether our shot had done any damage, beyond making the circular opening in the cloud curtain, we could not tell, for almost immediately the surrounding black smoke masses billowed in to fill up the hole.

But in the brief glimpse we had caught sight of two or three large air ships hovering in space above that part of the Lake of the Sun and its bordering city which we had beheld. It seemed to me in the brief glance I had that one ship had been touched by the discharge and was wandering in an erratic manner. But the clouds closed in so rapidly that I not be certain.

Penetrating the Cloud.

Anyhow, we had demonstrated one thing, and that was that we could penetrate the cloud shield and reach the Martians in their hiding place.

It had been prearranged that the first discharge from the flagship should be a signal for the concentration of the fire of all the other ships upon the same spot.

A little hesitation, however, occurred, and a half a minute had elapsed before the disintegrators from the other members of the squadron were got into play.

The Martians' Artificial Day.

Then, suddenly we saw an immense commotion in the cloud beneath us. It seemed to be beaten and hurled in every direction and punctured like a sieve with nearly a hundred great circular holes. Through these gaps we could see clearly a large region of the planet's surface, with many airships floating above it, and the blaze of innumerable electric lights illuminating it. The Martians had created an artificial day under the curtain.

This time there was no question that the blow had been effective. Four or five of the airships, partially destroyed, tumbled headlong toward the ground, while even from our great distance there was unmistakable evidence that fearful execution had been done among the crowded structures along the shore of the Lake.

Our Disintegrator Does Awful Damage.

Four or five of the airships tumbled headlong toward the ground, and it was evident that fearful execution had been done among the crowded structures along the shore of the lake.

As each of our ships possessed but one of the new disintegrators, and since a minute or so was required to adjust them for a fresh discharge, we remained for a little while inactive after delivering the blow. Meanwhile the cloud curtain, though rent to shreds by the concentrated discharge of the disintegrators, quickly became a uniform black sheet again, hiding everything.

We had just had time to congratulate ourselves on the successful opening of our bombardment, and the disintegrator of the flagship was poised for another discharge, when suddenly out of the black expanse beneath, quivered immense electric beams, clear cut and straight as bars of steel, but dazzling our eyes with unendurable brilliance.

It was the reply of the Martians to our attack.

Devastating Our Army.

Three or four of the electrical ships were seriously damaged, and one, close beside the flagship, changed color, withered and collapsed, with the same sickening phenomena that had made our hearts shudder when the first disaster of this kind occurred during our brief battle over the asteroid.

Another score of our comrades were gone, and yet we had hardly begun the fight.

Glancing at the other ships, which had been injured, I saw that the damage to them was not so serious, although they were evidently hors de combat for the present.

Our fighting blood was now boiling and we did not stop long to count our losses.

"Into the smoke!" was the signal, and the ninety and more electric ships which still remained in condition for action immediately shot downward.

Chapter XI

A Dash Into the Smoke.

It was a wild plunge. We kept off the decks while rushing through the blinding smoke, but the instant we emerged below, where we found ourselves still a mile above the ground, we were out again, ready to strike.

I have simply a confused recollection of flashing lights beneath, and a great, dark arch of clouds above, out of which our ships seemed dropping on all sides, and then the fray burst upon and around us, and no man could see or notice anything except by half-comprehended glances.

Almost in an instant, it seemed, a swarm of airships surrounded us, while from what, for lack of a more descriptive name, I shall call the forts about the Lake of the Sun, leaped tongues of electric fire, before which some of our ships were driven like bits of flaming paper in a high wind, gleaming for a moment, then curling up and gone forever!

Never Was Such a Conflict.

It was an awful sight; but the battle fever was raging in us, and we, on our part, were not idle.

Every man carried a disintegrator, and these hand instruments, together with those of heavier calibre on the ships poured their resistless vibrations in every direction through the quivering air.

The airships of the Martians were destroyed by the score, but yet they flocked upon us thicker and faster.

We dropped lower and our blows fell upon the forts, and upon the wide-spread city bordering the Lake of the Sun. We almost entirely silenced the fire of one of the forts; but there were forty more in full action within reach of our eyes!

Some of the metallic buildings were partly unroofed by the disintegrators and some had their walls riddled and fell with thundering crashes, whose sound rose to our ears above the hellish din of battle. I caught glimpses of giant forms struggling in the ruins and rushing wildly through the streets, but there was no time to see anything clearly.

The Flagship Charmed!

Our flagship seemed charmed. A crowd of airships hung upon it like a swarm of angry bees, and, at times, one could not see for the lightning strokes—yet we escaped destruction, while ourselves dealing death on every hand.

It was a glorious fight, but it was not war; no, it was not war. We really had no more chance of ultimate success amid that multitude of enemies than a prisoner running the gauntlet in a crowd of savages has of escape.

A conviction of the hopelessness of the contest finally forced itself upon our minds, and the shattered squadron, which had kept well together amid the storm of death, was signalled to retreat.

Shaking off their pursuers, as a hunted bear shakes off the dogs, sixty of the electrical ships rose up through the clouds where more than ninety had gone down!

Madly we rushed upward through the vast curtain and continued our flight to a great elevation, far beyond the reach of the awful artillery of the enemy.

Forced to Retreat.

Looking back it seemed the very mouth of hell that we had escaped from.

The Martians did not for an instant cease their fire, even when we were far beyond their reach. With furious persistence they blazed away through the cloud curtains, and the vivid spikes of lightning shuddered so swiftly on one another's track that they were like a flaming halo of electric lances around the frowning helmet of the War Planet.

But after a while they stopped their terrific sparring, and once more the immense globe assumed the appearance of a vast ball of black smoke, still wildly agitated by the recent disturbance, but exhibiting no opening through which we could discern what was going on beneath.

Evidently the Martians believed they had finished us.

Despair Seizes Us.

At no time since the beginning of our adventure had it appeared to me quite so hopeless, reckless and mad as it seemed at present.

We had suffered fearful losses, and yet what had we accomplished? We had won two fights on the asteroid, it is true, but then we had overwhelming numbers on our side.

Now we were facing millions on their own ground, and our very first assault had resulted in a disastrous repulse, with the loss of at least thirty electric ships and 600 men!

Evidently we could not endure this sort of thing. We must find some other means of assailing Mars or else give up the attempt.

But the latter was not to be thought of. It was no mere question of self-pride, however, and no consideration of the tremendous interests at stake, which would compel us to continue our apparently vain attempt.

No Hope in Sight.

Our provisions could last only a few days longer. The supply would not carry us one-quarter of the way back to the earth, and we must therefore remain here and literally conquer or die.

In this extremity a consultation of the principal officers was called upon the deck of the flagship.

Here the suggestion was made that we should attempt to effect by strategy what we had failed to do by force.

An old army officer who had served in many wars against the cunning Indians of the West, Colonel Alonzo Jefferson Smith, was the author of this suggestion.

"Let us circumvent them," he said. "We can do it in this way. The chances are that all of the available fighting force of the planet Mars is now concentrated on this side and in the neighborhood of the Lake of the Sun."

Formulating a "Last Hope."

"Possibly, by some kind of X-ray business, they can only see us dimly through the clouds, and if we get a little further away they will not be able to see us at all."

"Now, I suggest that a certain number of the electrical ships be withdrawn from the squadron to a great distance, while the remainder stay here; or, better still, approach to a point just beyond the reach of those streaks of lightning, and begin a bombardment of the clouds without paying any attention to whether the strokes reach through the clouds and do any damage or not."

"This will induce the Martians to believe that we are determined to press our attack at this point."

"In the meantime, while these ships are raising a hullabaloo on this side of the planet, and drawing their fire, as much as possible, without running into any actual danger, let the others which have been selected for the purpose, sail rapidly around to the other side of Mars and take them in the rear."

It was not perfectly clear what Colonel Smith intended to do after the landing had been effected in the rear of the Martians, but still there seemed a good deal to be said for his suggestion, and it would, at any rate, if carried out, enable us to learn something about the condition of things on the planet, and perhaps furnish us with a hint as to how we could best proceed in the further prosecution of the siege.

Accordingly it was resolved that about twenty ships should be told off for this movement, and Colonel Smith himself was placed in command.

At my desire I accompanied the new commander in his flagship.

Flank Movements.

Rising to a considerable elevation in order that there might be no risk of being seen, we began our flank movement while the remaining ships, in accordance with the understanding, dropped nearer the curtain of cloud and commenced a bombardment with the disintegrators, which caused a tremendous commotion in the clouds, opening vast gaps in them, and occasionally revealing a glimpse of the electric lights on the planet, although it was evident that the vibratory currents did not reach the ground. The Martians immediately replied to this renewed attack, and again the cloud-covered globe bristled with lightning, which flashed so fiercely out of the blackness below that the stoutest hearts among us quailed, although we were situated well beyond the danger.

But this sublime spectacle rapidly vanished from our eyes when, having attained a proper elevation, we began our course toward the opposite hemisphere of the planet.

We guided our flight by the stars, and from our knowledge of the rotation period of Mars, and the position which the principal points on its surface must occupy at certain hours, we were able to tell what part of the planet lay beneath us.

Having completed our semi-circuit, we found ourselves on the night side of Mars, and determined to lose no time in executing our coup. But it was deemed best that an exploration should first be made by a single electrical ship, and Colonel Smith naturally wished to undertake the adventure with his own vessel.

Dropping to the Planet.

We dropped rapidly through the black cloud curtain, which proved to be at least half a mile in thickness, and then suddenly emerged, as if suspended at the apex of an enormous dome, arching above the surface of the planet a mile beneath us, which sparkled on all sides with innumerable lights.

These lights were so numerous and so brilliant as to produce a faint imitation of daylight, even at our immense height above the ground, and the dome of cloud out of which we had emerged assumed a soft fawn color that produced an indescribably beautiful effect.

For a moment we recoiled from our undertaking, and arrested the motion of the electric ship.

But on closely examining the surface beneath us we found that there was a broad region, where comparatively few bright lights were to be seen. From my knowledge of the geography of Mars I knew that this was a part of the Land of Ausonia, situated a few hundred miles northeast of Hellas, where we had first seen the planet.

Evidently it was not so thickly populated as some of the other parts of Mars, and its comparative darkness was an attraction to us. We determined to approach within a few hundred feet of the ground with the electric ship, and then, in case no enemies appeared, to visit the soil itself.

"Perhaps we shall see or hear something that will be of use to us," said Colonel Smith, "and for the purposes of this first reconnaissance it is better that we should be few in number. The other ships will await our return, and at any rate we shall not be gone long."

As our car approached the ground we found ourselves near the tops of some lofty trees.

"This will do," said Colonel Smith, to the electrical steersman. "Stay right here."

He and I then lowered ourselves into the branches of the trees, each carrying a small disintegrator, and cautiously clambered down to the ground.

Landing On Mars.

We believed we were the first of the descendants of Adam to set foot on the planet of Mars.

An Experience On Mars.

The Great Planet Exhibits Its Wonders to Our Warriors.

At first we suffered somewhat from the effects of the rare atmosphere. It was so lacking in density that it resembled the air on the summits of the loftiest terrestrial mountains.

Having reached the foot of the tree in safety, we lay down for a moment on the ground to recover ourselves and to become accustomed to our new surroundings.

A thrill, born half of wonder, half of incredulity, ran through me at the touch of the soil of Mars. Here was I, actually on that planet, which had seemed so far away, so inaccessible, and so full of mysteries when viewed from the earth. And yet, surrounding me, were things—gigantic, it is true—but still resembling and recalling the familiar sights of my own world.

After a little while our lungs became accustomed to the rarity of the atmosphere and we experienced a certain stimulation in breathing.

Starting on our Travels.

We then got upon our feet and stepped out from under the shadow of the gigantic tree. High above we could faintly see our electrical ship, gently swaying in the air close to the treetop.

There were no electric lights in our immediate neighborhood, but we noticed that the whole surface of the planet around us was gleaming with them, producing an effect like the glow of a great city seen from a distance at night. The glare was faintly reflected from the vast dome of clouds above, producing the general impression of a moonlight night upon the earth.

It was a wonderfully quiet and beautiful spot where we had come down. The air had a delicate feel and a bracing temperature, while a soft breeze soughed through the leaves of the tree above our heads.

Not far away was the bank of a canal, bordered by a magnificent avenue shaded by a double row of immense umbrageous trees.

We approached the canal, and, getting upon the road, turned to the left to make an exploration in that direction. The shadow of the trees falling upon the roadway produced a dense gloom, in the midst of which we felt that we should be safe, unless the Martians had eyes like those of cats.

An Alarming Encounter.

As we pushed along, our hearts, I confess, beating a little quickly, a shadow stirred in front of us.

Something darker than the night itself approached.

As it drew near it assumed the appearance of an enormous dog, as tall as an ox, which ran swiftly our way with a threatening motion of its head. But before it could even utter a snarl the whirr of Colonel Smith's disintegrator was heard and the creature vanished in the shadow.

"Gracious, did you ever see such a beast?" said the Colonel. "Why, he was as big as a grizzly."

"The people he belonged to must be near by," I said. "Very likely he was a watch on guard."

"But I see no signs of a habitation."

"True, but you observe there is a thick hedge on the side of the road opposite the canal. If we get through that perhaps we shall catch sight of something."

A Palace in View.

Cautiously we pushed our way through the hedge, which was composed of shrubs as large as small trees, and very thick at the bottom, and, having traversed it, found ourselves in a great meadow-like expanse which might have been a lawn. At a considerable distance, in the midst of a clump of trees, a large building towered skyward, its walls of some red metal, gleaming like polished copper in the soft light that fell from the cloud dome.

There were no lights around the building itself, and we saw nothing corresponding to windows on that side which faced us, but toward the right a door was evidently open, and out of this streamed a brilliant shaft of illumination, which lay bright upon the lawn, then crossed the highway through an opening in the hedge, and gleamed on the water of the canal beyond.

Where we stood the ground had evidently been recently cleared, and there was no obstruction, but as we crept closer to the house—for our curiosity had now become irresistible—we found ourselves crawling through grass so tall that if we had stood erect it would have risen well above our heads.

Taking Precautions.

"This affords good protection," said Colonel Smith, recalling his adventures on the Western plains. "We can get close in to the Indians—I beg pardon, I mean the Martians—without being seen."

Heavens, what an adventure was this! To be crawling about in the night on the face of another world and venturing, perhaps, into the jaws of a danger which human experience could not measure!

But on we went, and in a little while we had emerged from the tall grass and were somewhat startled by the discovery that we had got close to the wall of the building.

Carefully we crept around toward the open door.

As we neared it we suddenly stopped as if we had been stricken with instantaneous paralysis.

Out of the door floated, on the soft night air, the sweetest music I have ever listened to.

A Monstrous Surprise.

It carried me back in an instant to my own world. It was the music of the earth. It was the melodious expression of a human soul. It thrilled us both to the heart's core.

"My God!" exclaimed Colonel Smith. "What can that be? Are we dreaming, or where in heaven's name are we?"

Still the enchanting harmony floated out upon the air.

What the instrument was I could not tell; but the sound seemed more nearly to resemble that of a violin than of anything else I could think of.

Magnificent Music.

When we first heard it the strains were gentle, sweet, caressing and full of an infinite depth of feeling, but in a little while its tone changed, and it became a magnificent march, throbbing upon the air in stirring notes that set our hearts beating in unison with its stride and inspiring in us a courage that we had not felt before.

Then it drifted into a wild fantasia, still inexpressibly sweet, and from that changed again into a requiem or lament, whose mellifluous tide of harmony swept our thoughts back again to the earth.

"I can endure this no longer," I said. "I must see who it is that makes that music. It is the product of a human heart and must come from the touch of human fingers."

We carefully shifted our position until we stood in the blaze of light that poured out of the door.

The doorway was an immense arched opening, magnificently ornamented, rising to a height of, I should say, not less than twenty or twenty-five feet and broad in proportion. The door itself stood widely open and it, together with all of its fittings and surroundings, was composed of the same beautiful red metal.

A Beautiful Girl!

Stepping out a little way into the light I could see within the door an immense apartment, glittering on all sides with metallic ornaments and gems and lighted from the centre by a great chandelier of electric candles.

In the middle of the great floor, holding the instrument delicately poised, and still awaking its ravishing voice, stood a figure, the sight of which almost stopped my breath.

It was a slender sylph of a girl!

A girl of my own race: a human being here upon the planet Mars!

A Beautiful Human Girl Discovered on Mars.

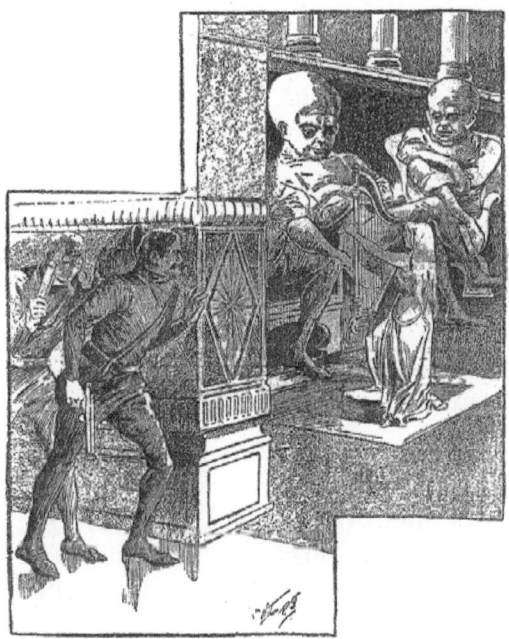

In the middle of the great floor, holding the instrument delicately poised, and still awaking its ravishing voice, stood a figure, the sight of which almost stopped my breath! It was a slender sylph of a girl! A girl of my own race; a human being here on Mars!

Her hair was loosely coiled and she was attired in graceful white drapery.

"By ——!" cried Colonel Smith, "she's human!"

Chapter XII

Still the bewildering strains of the music came to our ears, and yet we stood there unperceived, though in the full glare of the chandelier.

The girl's face was presented in profile. It was exquisite in beauty, pale, delicate with a certain pleading sadness which stirred us to the heart.

An element of romance and a touch of personal interest such as we had not looked for suddenly entered into our adventure.

Colonel Smith's mind still ran back to the perils of the plains.

A Human Prisoner.

"She is a prisoner," he said, "and by the Seven Devils of Dona Ana we'll not leave her here. But where are the hellhounds themselves?"

Our attention had been so absorbed by the sight of the girl that we had scarcely thought of looking to see if there was any one else in the room.

Glancing beyond her, I now perceived sitting in richly decorated chairs three or four gigantic Martians. They were listening to the music as if charmed.

The whole story told itself. This girl, if not their slave, was at any rate under their control, and she was furnishing entertainment for them by her musical skill. The fact that they could find pleasure in music so beautiful was, perhaps, an indication that they were not really as savage as they seemed.

Yet our hearts went out to the girl, and were turned against them with an uncontrollable hatred.

They were of the same remorseless race with those who so lately had lain waste our fair earth and who would have completed its destruction had not Providence interfered in our behalf.

Singularly enough, although we stood full in the light, they had not yet seen us.

Martians Guarding Her.

Suddenly the girl, moved by what impulse I know not, turned her face in our direction. Her eyes fell upon us. She paused abruptly in her playing, and her instrument dropped to the floor. Then she uttered a cry, and with extended arms ran toward us.

But when she was near she stopped abruptly, the glad look fading from her face, and started back with terror-stricken eyes, as if, after all, she had found us not what she expected.

Then for an instant she looked more intently at us, her countenance cleared once more, and, overcome by some strange emotion, her eyes filled with tears, and, drawing a little nearer, she stretched forth her hands to us appealingly.

Meanwhile the Martians had started to their feet. They looked down upon us in astonishment. We were like pigmies to them; like little gnomes which had sprung out of the ground at their feet.

One of the giants seized some kind of a weapon and started forward with a threatening gesture.

The Girl Appeals to Us.

The girl sprang to my side and grasped my arm with a cry of fear.

This seemed to throw the Martian into a sudden frenzy, and he raised his arms to strike.

But the disintegrator was in my hand.

My rage was equal to his.

I felt the concentrated vengeance of the earth quivering through me as I pressed the button of the disintegrator and, sweeping it rapidly up and down, saw the gigantic form that confronted me melt into nothingness.

There were three other giants in the room, and they had been on the point of following up the attack of their comrade. But when he disappeared from before their eyes, they paused, staring in amazement at the place where, but a moment before, he had stood, but where now only the metal weapon he had wielded lay on the floor.

At first they started back, and seemed on the point of fleeing; then, with a second glance, perceiving again how small and insignificant we were, all three together advanced upon us.

The girl sank trembling on her knees.

In the meantime I had readjusted my disintegrator for another discharge, and Colonel Smith stood by me with the light of battle upon his face.

"Sweep the discharge across the three," I exclaimed. "Otherwise there will be one left and before we can fire again he will crush us."

The Martians Are Killed.

The whirr of the two instruments sounded simultaneously, and with a quick, horizontal motion we swept the lines of force around in such a manner that all three of the Martians were caught by the vibratory streams and actually cut in two.

Long gaps were opened in the wall of the room behind them, where the destroying currents had passed, for with wrathful fierceness, we had run the vibrations through half a gamut on the index.

The victory was ours. There were no other enemies, that we could see, in the house.

Yet at any moment others might make their appearance, and what more we did must be done quickly.

The girl evidently was as much amazed as the Martians had been by the effects which we had produced. Still she was not terrified, and continued to cling to us and to glance beseechingly into our faces, expressing in her every look and gesture the fact that she knew we were of her own race.

But clearly she could not speak our tongue, for the words she uttered were unintelligible.

Colonel Smith, whose long experience in Indian warfare had made him intensely practical, did not lose his military instincts, even in the midst of events so strange.

"It occurs to me," he said, "that we have got a chance at the enemies' supplies. Suppose we begin foraging right here. Let's see if this girl can't show us the commissary department."

He immediately began to make signs to the girl to indicate that he was hungry.

The Girl Understands Us.

A look of comprehension flitted over her features, and, seizing our hands, she led us into an adjoining apartment and pointed to a number of metallic boxes. One of these she opened, taking out of it a kind of cake, which she placed between her teeth, breaking off a very small portion and then handing it to us, motioning that we should eat, but at the same time showing us that we ought to take only a small quantity.

"Thank God! It's compressed food," said Colonel Smith. "I thought these Martians with their wonderful civilization would be up to that. And it's mighty lucky for us, because, without overburdening ourselves, if we can find one or two more caches like this we shall be able to reprovision the entire fleet. But we must get reinforcements before we can take possession of the fodder."

The Prisoner Is Rescued.

Accordingly we hurried out into the night, passed into the roadway, and, taking the girl with us, ran as rapidly as possible to the foot of the tree where we had made our descent. Then we signalled to the electric ship to drop down to the level of the ground.

This was quickly done, the girl was taken aboard, and a dozen men, under our guidance, hastened back to the house, where we loaded ourselves with the compressed provisions and conveyed them to the ship.

Beautiful Girl Prisoner.

Establishing the Identity of the Martians' Captive.

On this second trip to the mysterious house we had discovered another apartment containing a very large number of the metallic boxes, filled with compressed food.

"By Jove, it is a store house," said Colonel Smith. "We must get more force and carry it all off. Gracious, but this is a lucky night. We can reprovision the whole fleet from this room."

Taking Compressed Food From the Martians.

"By Jove! It is a storehouse," said Colonel Smith. "We must carry the food off. We can provision the whole fleet from this room!"

"I thought it singular," I said, "that with the exception of the girl whom we have rescued no women were seen in the house. Evidently the lights over yonder indicate the location of a considerable town, and it is quite probable that this building, without windows, and so strongly constructed, is the common storehouse, where the provisions for the town are kept. The fellows we killed must have been the watchmen in charge of the storehouse, and they were treating themselves to a little music from the slave girl when we happened to come upon them."

A New Food Supply.

With the utmost haste several of the other electrical ships, waiting above the cloud curtain, were summoned to descend, and, with more than a hundred men, we returned to the building, and this time almost entirely exhausted its stores, each man carrying as much as he could stagger under.

Fortunately our proceedings had been conducted without much noise, and the storehouse being situated at a considerable distance from other buildings, none of the Martians, except those who would never tell the story, had known of our arrival or of our doings on the planet.

"Now, we'll return and surprise Edison with the news," said Colonel Smith.

Our ship was the last to pass up through the clouds, and it was a strange sight to watch the others as one after another they rose toward the great dome, entered it, though from below it resembled a solid vault of grayish-pink marble, and disappeared.

Sunshine Again.

We quickly followed them, and having penetrated the enormous curtain, were considerably surprised on emerging at the upper side to find that the sun was shining brilliantly upon us. It will be remembered that it was night on this side of Mars when we went down, but our adventure had occupied several hours, and now Mars had so far turned upon its axis that the portion of its surface over which we were had come around into the sunlight.

We knew that the squadron which we had left besieging the Lake of the Sun must also have been carried around in a similar manner, passing into the night while the side of the planet where we were was emerging into day.

Our shortest way back would be by travelling westward, because then we should be moving in a direction opposite to that in which the planet rotated, and the main squadron, sharing that rotation, would be continually moving in our direction.

But to travel westward was to penetrate once more into the night side of the planet.

The prows, if I may so call them, of our ships were accordingly turned in the direction of the vast shadow which Mars was invisibly projecting into space behind it, and on entering that shadow the sun disappeared from our eyes, and once more the huge hidden globe beneath us became a black chasm among the stars.

Now that we were in the neighborhood of a globe capable of imparting considerable weight to all things under the influence of its attraction that peculiar condition which I have before described as existing in the midst of space, where there was neither up nor down for us, had ceased. Here where we had weight "up" and "down" had resumed their old meanings. "Down" was toward the centre of Mars, and "up" was away from that centre.

The Two Moons of Mars.

Standing on the deck, and looking overhead as we swiftly ploughed our smooth way at a great height through the now imperceptible atmosphere of the planet, I saw the two moons of Mars meeting in the sky exactly above us.

Before our arrival at Mars, there had been considerable discussion among the learned men as to the advisability of touching at one of their moons, and when the discovery was made that our provisions were nearly exhausted, it had been suggested that the Martian satellites might furnish us with an additional supply.

But it had appeared a sufficient reply to this suggestion that the moons of Mars are both insignificant bodies, not much larger than the asteroid we had fallen in with, and that there could not possibly be any form of vegetation or other edible products upon them.

This view having prevailed, we had ceased to take an interest in the satellites, further than to regard them as objects of great curiosity on account of their motions.

The nearer of these moons, Phobos, is only 3,700 miles from the surface of Mars, and we watched it travelling around the planet three times in the course of every day. The more distant one, Deimos, 12,500 miles away, required considerably more than one day to make its circuit.

It now happened that the two had come into conjunction, as I have said, just over our heads, and, throwing myself down on my back on the deck of the electrical ship, for a long time I watched the race between the two satellites, until Phobos, rapidly gaining upon the other, had left its rival far behind.

Suddenly Colonel Smith, who took very little interest in these astronomical curiosities, touched me, and pointing ahead, said:

"There they are."

Rejoining the Fleet.

I looked, and sure enough there were the signal lights of the principal squadron, and as we gazed we occasionally saw, darting up from the vast cloud mass beneath, an electric bayonet, fiercely thrust into the sky, which showed that the siege was still actively going on, and that the Martians were jabbing away at their invisible enemies outside the curtain.

In a short time the two fleets had joined, and Colonel Smith and I immediately transferred ourselves to the flagship.

"Well, what have you done?" asked Mr. Edison, while others crowded around with eager attention.

"If we have not captured their provision train," said Colonel Smith, "we have done something just about as good. We have foraged on the country, and have collected a supply that I reckon will last this fleet for at least a month."

"What's that? What's that?"

"It's just what I say," and Colonel Smith brought out of his pocket one of the square cakes of compressed food. "Set your teeth in that, and see what you think of it, but don't take too much, for it's powerful strong."

"I say," he continued, "we have got enough of that stuff to last us all for a month, but we've done more than that; we have got a surprise for you that will make you open your eyes. Just wait a minute."

Caring for the Rescued Girl.

Colonel Smith made a signal to the electrical ship which we had just quitted to draw near. It came alongside, so that one could step from its deck onto the flagship. Colonel Smith disappeared for a minute in the interior of his ship, then re-emerged, leading the girl whom we had found upon the planet.

"Take her inside, quick," he said, "for she is not used to this thin air."

In fact, we were at so great an elevation that the rarity of the atmosphere now compelled us all to wear our air-tight suits, and the girl, not being thus attired, would have fallen unconscious on the deck if we had not instantly removed her to the interior of the car.

There she quickly recovered from the effects of the deprivation of air and looked about her, pale, astonished, but yet apparently without fear.

Every motion of this girl convinced me that she not only recognized us as members of her own race, but that she felt that her only hope lay in our aid. Therefore, strange as we were to her in many respects, nevertheless she did not think that she was in danger while among us.

The circumstances under which we had found her were quickly explained. Her beauty, her strange fate and the impenetrable mystery which surrounded her excited universal admiration and wonder.

How Came She on Mars?

"How did she get on Mars?" was the question that everybody asked, and that nobody could answer.

But while all were crowding around and overwhelming the poor girl with their staring, suddenly she burst into tears, and then, with arms outstretched in the same appealing manner which had so stirred our sympathies when we first saw her in the house of the Martians, she broke forth in a wild recitation, which was half a song and half a wail.

As she went on I noticed that a learned professor of languages from the University of Heidelberg was listening to her with intense attention. Several times he appeared to be on the point of breaking in with an exclamation. I could plainly see that he was becoming more and more excited as the words poured from the girl's lips. Occasionally he nodded and muttered, smiling to himself. Her song finished, the girl sank half-exhausted upon the floor. She was lifted and placed in a reclining position at the side of the car.

Then the Heidelberg professor stepped to the centre of the car, in the sight of all, and in a most impressive manner said:

"Gentlemen, our sister."

"I have her tongue recognized! The language that she speaks, the roots of the great Indo-European, or Aryan stock, contains."

"This girl, gentlemen, to the oldest family of the human race belongs. Her language every tongue that now upon the earth is spoken antedates. Convinced am I that it that great original speech is from which have all the languages of the civilized world sprung."

"How she here came, so many millions of miles from the earth, a great mystery is. But it shall be penetrated, and it is from her own lips that we the truth shall learn, because not difficult to us shall it be the language that she speaks to acquire since to our own it is akin."

The Professor's Astonishing Statement.

This announcement of the Heidelberg professor stirred us all most profoundly. It not only deepened our interest in the beautiful girl whom we had rescued, but, in a dim way, it gave us reason to hope that we should yet discover some means of mastering the Martians by dealing them a blow from within.

It had been expected, the reader will remember, that the Martian whom we had made prisoner on the asteroid, might be of use to us in a similar way, and for that reason great efforts had been made to acquire his language, and considerable progress had been effected in that direction.

But from the moment of our arrival at Mars itself, and especially after the battles began, the prisoner had resumed his savage and uncommunicative disposition, and had seemed continually to be expecting that we would fall victims to the prowess of his fellow beings, and that he would be released. How an outlaw, such as he evidently was, who had been caught in the act of robbing the Martian gold mines, could expect to escape punishment on returning to his native planet it was difficult to see. Nevertheless, so strong are the ties of race we could plainly perceive that all his sympathies were for his own people.

In fact, in consequence of his surly manner, and his attempts to escape, he had been more strictly bound than before and to get him out of the way had been removed from the flagship, which was already overcrowded, and placed in one of the other electric ships, and this ship—as it happened—was one of those which were lost in the great battle beneath the clouds. So after all, the Martian had perished, by a vengeful stroke launched from his native globe.

But Providence had placed in our hands a far better interpreter than he could ever have been. This girl of our own race would need no urging, or coercion, on our part in order to induce her to reveal any secrets of the Martians that might be useful in our further proceedings.

But one thing was first necessary to be done.

We must learn to talk with her.

Learning Her Language.

But for the discovery of the store of provisions it would have been impossible for us to spare the time needed to acquire the language of the girl, but now that we had been saved from the danger of starvation, we could prolong the siege for several weeks, employing the intervening time to the best advantage.

The terrible disaster which we had suffered in the great battle above the Lake of the Sun, wherein we had lost nearly a third of our entire force, had been quite sufficient to convince us that our only hope of victory lay in dealing the Martians some paralyzing stroke that at one blow would deprive them of the power of resistance. A victory that cost us the loss of a single ship would be too dearly purchased now.

How to deal that blow, and first of all, how to discover the means of dealing it, were at present the uppermost problems in our minds.

The only hope for us lay in the girl.

If, as there was every reason to believe, she was familiar with the ways and secrets of the Martians, then she might be able to direct our efforts in such a manner as to render them effective.

"We can spare two weeks for this," said Mr. Edison. "Can you fellows of many tongues learn to talk with the girl in that time?"

"We'll try it," said several.

"It shall we do," cried the Heidelberg professor more confidently.

"Then there is no use of staying here," continued the commander. "If we withdraw the Martians will think that we have either given up the contest or been destroyed. Perhaps they will then pull off their blanket and let us see their face once more.

That will give us a better opportunity to strike effectively when we are again ready."

Preparing a Rendezvous.

"Why not rendezvous at one of the moons?" said an astronomer. "Neither of the two moons is of much consequence, as far as size goes, but still it would serve as a sort of anchorage ground, and while there, if we were careful to keep on the side away from Mars, we should escape detection."

This suggestion was immediately accepted, and the squadron having been signalled to assemble quickly bore off in the direction of the more distant moon of Mars, Deimos. We knew that it was slightly smaller than Phobos but its greater distance gave promise that it would better serve our purpose of temporary concealment. The moons of Mars, like the earth's moon, always keep the same face toward their master. By hiding behind Deimos we should escape the prying eyes of the Martians, even when they employed telescopes, and thus be able to remain comparatively close at hand, ready to pounce down upon them again after we had obtained, as we now had good hope of doing, information that would make us masters of the situation.

Chapter XIII

On One of Mars' Moons.

Deimos proved to be, as we had expected, about six miles in diameter. Its mean density is not very great so that the acceleration of gravity did not exceed one two-thousandths of the earth's. Consequently the weight of a man turning the scales at 150 pounds at home was here only about one ounce.

The result was that we could move about with greater ease than on the golden asteroid, and some of the scientific men eagerly resumed their interrupted experiments.

But the attraction of this little satellite was so slight that we had to be very careful not to move too swiftly in going about lest we should involuntarily leave the ground and sail out into space, as, it will be remembered, happened to the fugitives during the fight on the asteroid.

Not only would such an adventure have been an uncomfortable experience, but it might have endangered the success of our scheme. Our present distance from the surface of Mars did not exceed 12,500 miles, and we had reason to believe that Martians possessed telescopes powerful enough to enable them not merely to see the electrical ships at such a distance, but to also catch sight of us individually. Although the cloud curtain still rested on the planet it was probable that the Martians would send some of their airships up to its surface in order to determine what our fate had been. From that point of vantage, with their exceedingly powerful glasses, we feared that they might be able to detect anything unusual upon or in the neighborhood of Deimos.

The Ships are Moored.

Accordingly strict orders were given, not only that the ships should be moored on that side of the satellite which is perpetually turned away from Mars, but that, without orders, no one should venture around on the other side of the little globe, or even on the edge of it, where he might be seen in profile against the sky.

Still, of course, it was essential that we, on our part, should keep a close watch, and so a number of sentinels were selected, whose duty it was to place themselves at the edge of Deimos, where they could peep over the horizon, so to speak, and catch sight of the globe of our enemies.

The distance of Mars from us was only about three times its own diameter, consequently it shut off a large part of the sky, as viewed from our position.

But in order to see its whole surface it was necessary to go a little beyond the edge of the satellite, on that side which faced Mars. At the suggestion of Colonel Smith, who had so frequently stalked Indians that devices of this kind readily occurred to his mind, the sentinels all wore garments corresponding in color to that of the soil of the asteroid, which was of a dark, reddish brown hue. This would tend to conceal them from the prying eyes of the Martians.

The commander himself frequently went around the edge of the planet in order to take a look at Mars, and I often accompanied him.

Marvellous Discoveries.

The Martians Were the Builders of the Great Sphinx and the Pyramids.

I shall never forget one occasion, when, lying flat on the ground, and cautiously worming our way around on the side toward Mars, we had just begun to observe it with our telescopes, when I perceived, against the vast curtain of smoke, a small, glinting object, which I instantly suspected to be an airship.

I called Mr. Edison's attention to it, and we both agreed that it was, undoubtedly, one of the Martians' aerial vessels, probably on the lookout for us.

A short time afterward a large number of airships made their appearance at the upper surface of the clouds, moving to and fro, and although, with our glasses, we could only make out the general form of the ships, without being able to discern the Martians upon them, yet we had not the least doubt but they were sweeping the sky in every direction in order to determine whether we had been completely destroyed or had retreated to a distance from the planet.

Even when that side of Mars on which we were looking had passed into night, we could still see the guardships circling above the clouds, their presence being betrayed by the faint twinkling of the electric lights that they bore.

Finally, after about a week had passed, the Martians evidently made up their minds that they had annihilated us, and that there was no longer danger to be feared. Convincing evidence that they believed we should not be heard from again was furnished when the withdrawal of the great curtain of cloud began.

A Great Phenomenon.

This phenomenon first manifested itself by a gradual thinning of the vaporous shield, until, at length, we began to perceive the red surface of the planet dimly shining through it. Thinner and rarer it became, and, after the lapse of about eighteen hours, it had completely disappeared, and the huge globe shone out again, reflecting the light of the sun from its continents and oceans with a brightness that, in contrast with the all-enveloping night to which we had so long been subjected, seemed unbearable to our eyes.

Indeed, so brilliant was the illumination which fell upon the surface of Deimos that the number of persons who had been permitted to pass around upon the exposed side of the satellite was carefully restricted. In the blaze of light which had been suddenly poured upon us we felt somewhat like malefactors unexpectedly enveloped in the illumination of a policeman's dark lantern.

Meanwhile, the object which we had in view in retreating to the satellite was not lost sight of, and the services of the chief linguists of the expedition were again called into use for the purpose of acquiring a new language. The experiment was conducted in the flagship. The fact that this time it was not a monster belonging to an utterly alien race upon whom we were to experiment, but a beautiful daughter of our common Mother Eve, added zest and interest as well as the most confident hopes of success to the efforts of those who were striving to understand the accents of her tongue.

Lingual Difficulties Ahead.

Still the difficulty was very great, notwithstanding the conviction of the professors that her language would turn out to be a form of the great Indo-European speech from which the many tongues of civilized men upon the earth had been derived.

The learned men, to tell the truth, gave the poor girl no rest. For hours at a time they would ply her with interrogations by voice and by gesture, until, at length, wearied beyond endurance, she would fall asleep before their faces.

Then she would be left undisturbed for a little while, but the moment her eyes opened again the merciless professors flocked about her once more, and resumed the tedious iteration of their experiments.

Our Heidelberg professor was the chief inquisitor, and he revealed himself to us in a new and entirely unexpected light. No one could have anticipated the depth and variety of his resources. He placed himself in front of the girl and gestured and gesticulated, bowed, nodded, shrugged his shoulders, screwed his face into an infinite variety of expressions, smiled, laughed, scowled and accompanied all these dumb shows with posturings, exclamations, queries, only half expressed in words, and cadences which, by some ingenious manipulation of the tones of the voice, he managed to make as marvellous expressive of his desires.

He was a universal actor—comedian, tragedian, buffoon—all in one. There was no shade of human emotion which he did not seem capable of giving expression to.

The Professor Does His Best.

His every attitude was a symbol, and all his features became in quick succession types of thought and exponents of hidden feelings, while his inquisitive nose stood forth in the midst of their ceaseless play like a perpetual interrogation point that would have electrified the Sphinx into life, and set its stone lips gabbling answers and explanations.

The girl looked on, partly astonished, partly amused, and partly comprehending. Sometimes she smiled, and then the beauty of her face became most captivating. Occasionally she burst into a cheery laugh when the professor was executing some of his extraordinary gyrations before her.

It was a marvellous exhibition of what the human intellect, when all its powers are concentrated upon a single object, is capable of achieving. It seemed to me, as I looked at the performance, that if all the races of men, who had been stricken asunder at the foot of the Tower of Babel by the miracle which made the tongues of each to speak a language unknown to the others, could be brought together again at the foot of the same tower, with all the advantages which thousands of years of education had in the meantime imparted to them, they would be able, without any miracle, to make themselves mutually understood.

And it was evident that an understanding was actually growing between the girl and the professor. Their minds were plainly meeting, and when both had become focused upon the same point, it was perfectly certain that the object of the experiment would be attained.

Whenever the professor got from the girl an intelligent reply to his pantomimic inquiries, or whenever he believed that he got such a reply, it was immediately jotted down in the ever open notebook which he carried in his hand.

And then he would turn to us standing by, and with one hand on his heart, and the other sweeping grandly through the air, would make a profound bow and say:

"The young lady and I great progress make already. I have her words comprehended. We shall wondrous mysteries solve. Jawohl! Wunderlich! Make yourselves gentlemen easy. Of the human race the ancestral stem have I here discovered."

Once I glanced over a page of his notebook, and there I read this:

"Mars—Zahmor."

"Copper—Hayez."

"Sword—Anz."

"I jump—Altesna."

"I slay—Amoutha."

"I cut off a head—Ksutaskofa."

"I sleep—Zlcha."

"I love—Levza."

Aha, Professor Heidelberg!

When I saw this last entry I looked suspiciously at the professor.

Was he trying to make love without our knowing it to the beautiful captive from Mars?

If so, I felt certain that he would get himself into difficulty. She had made a deep impression upon every man in the flagship, and I knew that there was more than one of the younger men who would have promptly called him to account if they had suspected him of trying to learn from those beautiful lips the words, "I love."

I pictured to myself the state of mind of Colonel Alonzo Jefferson Smith if, in my place, he had glanced over the notebook and read what I had read.

And then I thought of another handsome young fellow in the flagship—Sidney Phillips—who, if mere actions and looks could make him so, had become exceedingly devoted to this long lost and happily recovered daughter of Eve.

In fact, I had already questioned within my own mind whether the peace would be strictly kept between Colonel Smith and Mr. Phillips, for the former had, to my knowledge, noticed the young fellow's adoring glances, and had begun to regard him out of the corners of his eyes as if he considered him no better than an Apache or a Mexican greaser.

Jealousy Crops Out.

"But what," I asked myself, "would be the vengeance that Colonel Smith would take upon this skinny professor from Heidelberg if he thought that he, taking advantage of his linguistic powers, had stepped in between him and the damsel whom he had rescued?"

However, when I took a second look at the professor, I became convinced that he was innocent of any such amorous intention, and that he had learned, or believed he had learned, the word for "love" simply in pursuance of the method by which he meant to acquire the language of the girl.

There was one thing which gave some of us considerable misgiving, and that was the question whether, after all, the language the professor was acquiring was really the girl's own tongue or one that she had learned from the Martians.

But the professor bade us rest easy on that point. He assured us, in the first place, that this girl could not be the only human being living upon Mars, but that she must have friends and relatives there. That being so, they unquestionably had a language of their own, which they spoke when they were among themselves. Here finding herself among beings belonging to her own race, she would naturally speak her own tongue and not that which she had acquired from the Martians.

"Moreover, gentlemen," he added, "I have in her speech many roots of the great Aryan tongue already recognized."

We were greatly relieved by this explanation, which seemed to all of us perfectly satisfactory.

Yet, really, there was no reason why one language should be any better than the other for our present purpose. In fact, it might be more useful to us to know the language of the Martians themselves. Still, we all felt that we should prefer to know her language rather than that of the monsters among whom she had lived.

Colonel Smith expressed what was in all our minds when, after listening to the reasoning of the Professor, he blurted out:

"Thank God, she doesn't speak any of their blamed lingo! By Jove, it would soil her pretty lips."

"But also that she speaks, too," said the man from Heidelberg, turning to Colonel Smith with a grin. "We shall both of them eventually learn."

A Tedious Language Lesson.

Three entire weeks were passed in this manner. After the first week the girl herself materially assisted the linguists in their efforts to acquire her speech.

At length the task was so far advanced that we could, in a certain sense, regard it as practically completed. The Heidelberg Professor declared that he had mastered the tongue of the ancient Aryans. His delight was unbounded. With prodigious industry he set to work, scarcely stopping to eat or sleep, to form a grammar of the language.

"You shall see," he said, "it will the speculations of my countrymen vindicate."

No doubt the Professor had an exaggerated opinion of the extent of his acquirements, but the fact remained that enough had been learned of the girl's language to enable him and several others to converse with her quite as readily as a person of good capacity who has studied under the instructions of a native teacher during a period of six months can converse in a foreign tongue.

Immediately almost every man in the squadron set vigorously at work to learn the language of this fair creature for himself. Colonel Smith and Sidney Phillips were neck and neck in the linguistic race.

One of the first bits of information which the Professor had given out was the name of the girl.

We Learn Her Name.

It was Aina (pronounced Ah-ee-na).

This news was flashed throughout the squadron, and the name of our beautiful captive was on the lips of all.

After that came her story. It was a marvellous narrative. Translated into our tongue it ran as follows:

"The traditions of my fathers, handed down for generations so many that no one can number them, declare that the planet of Mars was not the place of our origin."

"Ages and ages ago our forefathers dwelt on another and distant world that was nearer to the sun than this one is, and enjoyed brighter daylight than we have here."

"They dwelt—as I have often heard the story from my father, who had learned it by heart from his father, and he from his—in a beautiful valley that was surrounded by enormous mountains towering into the clouds and white about their tops with snow that never melted. In the valley were lakes, around which clustered the dwellings of our race."

"It was, the traditions say, a land wonderful for its fertility, filled with all things that the heart could desire, splendid with flowers and rich with luscious fruits."

"It was a land of music, and the people who dwelt in it were very happy."

While the girl was telling this part of her story the Heidelberg Professor became visibly more and more excited. Presently he could keep quiet no longer, and suddenly exclaimed, turning to us who were listening, as the words of the girl were interpreted for us by one of the other linguists:

"Gentlemen, it is the Vale of Cashmere! Has not my great countryman, Adelung, so declared? Has he not said that the Valley of Cashmere was the cradle of the human race already?"

"From the Valley of Cashmere to the planet Mars—what a romance!" exclaimed one of the bystanders.

Colonel Smith appeared to be particularly moved, and I heard him humming under his breath, greatly to my astonishment, for this rough soldier was not much given to poetry or music:

"Who has not heard of the Vale of Cashmere,
With its roses the brightest that earth ever gave;
Its temples, its grottoes, its fountains as clear,
As the love-lighted eyes that hang over the wave."

Mr. Sidney Phillips, standing by, and also catching the murmur of Colonel Smith's words, showed in his handsome countenance some indications of distress, as if he wished he had thought of those lines himself.

Aina Tells Her Story.

The girl resumed her narrative:

"Suddenly there dropped down out of the sky strange gigantic enemies, armed with mysterious weapons, and began to slay and burn and make desolate. Our forefathers could not withstand them. They seemed like demons, who had been sent from the abodes of evil to destroy our race."

"Some of the wise men said that this thing had come upon our people because they had been very wicked, and the gods in Heaven were angry. Some said they came from the moon, and some from the far-away stars. But of these things my forefathers knew nothing for a certainty."

"The destroyers showed no mercy to the inhabitants of the beautiful valley. Not content with making it a desert, they swept over other parts of the earth."

"The tradition says that they carried off from the valley, which was our native land, a large number of our people, taking them first into a strange country, where there were oceans of sand, but where a great river, flowing through the midst of the sands, created a narrow land of fertility. Here, after having slain and driven out the native inhabitants, they remained for many years, keeping our people, whom they had carried into captivity, as slaves."

"And in this Land of Sand, it is said, they did many wonderful works."

"They had been astonished at the sight of the great mountains which surrounded our valley, for on Mars there are no mountains, and after they came into the Land of Sand they built there with huge blocks of stone mountains in imitation of what they had seen, and used them for purposes that our people did not understand."

"Then, too, it is said they left there at the foot of these mountains that they had made a gigantic image of the great chief who led them in their conquest of our world."

At this point in the story the Heidelberg Professor again broke in, fairly trembling with excitement:

The Wonders of the Martians!

"Gentlemen, gentlemen," he cried, "is it that you do not understand? This Land of Sand and of a wonderful fertilizing river—what can it be? Gentlemen, it is Egypt! These mountains of rock that the Martians have erected, what are they? Gentlemen, they are the great mystery of the land of the Nile, the Pyramids. The gigantic statue of their leader that they at the foot of their artificial mountains have set up—gentlemen, what is that? It is the Sphinx!"

The Martians Built the Sphinx.

"Gentlemen," exclaimed the Professor, "these mountains of rock that the Martians built are the Pyramids of Egypt. The gigantic statue of their leader is The Great Sphinx!"

The Professor's agitation was so great that he could go no further. And indeed there was not one of us who did not fully share his excitement. To think that we should have come to the planet Mars to solve one of the standing mysteries of the earth, which had puzzled mankind and defied all their efforts at solution for so many centuries! Here, then, was the explanation of how those gigantic blocks that constitute the great Pyramid of Cheops had been swung to their lofty elevation. It was not the work of puny man, as many an engineer had declared that it could not be, but the work of these giants of Mars.

Aina's Wonderful Story.

The Martians' Beautiful Prisoner Recounts Her Marvellous Adventures.

Aina resumed her story.

"At length, our traditions say, a great pestilence broke out in the Land of Sand, and a partial vengeance was granted to us in the destruction of the larger number of our enemies. At last the giants who remained, fleeing before this scourge of the gods, used the mysterious means at their command, and, carrying our ancestors with them, returned to their own world, in which we have ever since lived."

"Then there are more of your people in Mars?" said one of the professors.

"Alas, no," replied Aina, her eyes filling with tears, "I alone am left."

For a few minutes she was unable to speak. Then she continued:

An Ancient Martian Conquest.

"What fury possessed them I do not know, but not long ago an expedition departed from the planet, the purpose of which, as it was noised about over Mars, was the conquest of a distant world. After a time a few survivors of that expedition returned. The story they told caused great excitement among our masters. They had been successful in their battles with the inhabitants of the world they had invaded, but as in the days of our forefathers, in the Land of Sand, a pestilence smote them, and but few survivors escaped."

"Not long after that, you, with your mysterious ships, appeared in the sky of Mars. Our masters studied you with their telescopes, and those who had returned from the unfortunate expedition declared that you were inhabitants of the world which they had invaded, come, doubtless, to take vengeance upon them."

"Some of my people who were permitted to look through the telescopes of the Martians, saw you also, and recognized you as members of their own race. There were several thousand of us, altogether, and we were kept by the Martians to serve them as slaves, and particularly to delight their ears with music, for our people have always been especially skilful in the playing of musical instruments, and in songs, and while the Martians have but little musical skill themselves, they are exceedingly fond of these things."

Awaiting a Rescue.

"Although Mars had completed not less than five thousand circuits about the sun since our ancestors were brought as prisoners to its surface, yet the memory of our distant home had never perished from the hearts of our race, and when we recognized you, as we believed, our own brothers, come to rescue us from long imprisonment, there was great rejoicing. The news spread from mouth to mouth, wherever we were in the houses and families of our masters. We seemed to be powerless to aid you or to communicate with you in any manner. Yet our hearts went out to you, as in your ships you hung above the planet, and preparations were secretly made by all the members of our race for your reception when, as we believed, would occur, you should effect a landing upon the planet and destroy our enemies."

"But in some manner the fact that we had recognized you, and were preparing to welcome you, came to the ears of the Martians."

At this point the girl suddenly covered her eyes with her hands, shuddering and falling back in her seat.

"Oh, you do not know them as I do!" at length she exclaimed. "The monsters! Their vengeance was too terrible! Instantly the order went forth that we should all be butchered, and that awful command was executed!"

"How, then, did you escape?" asked the Heidelberg Professor.

Aina seemed unable to speak for a while. Finally mastering her emotion, she replied:

Her Fortunate Escape.

"One of the chief officers of the Martians wished me to remain alive. He, with his aides, carried me to one of the military depot of supplies, where I was found and rescued," and as she said this she turned toward Colonel Smith with a smile that reflected on his ruddy face and made it glow like a Chinese lantern.

"By ——!" muttered Colonel Smith, "that was the fellow we blew into nothing! Blast him, he got off too easy!"

The remainder of Aina's story may be briefly told.

When Colonel Smith and I entered the mysterious building which, as it now proved, was not a storehouse belonging to a village, as we had supposed, but one of the military depots of the Martians, the girl, on catching sight of us, immediately recognized us as belonging to the strange squadron in the sky. As such she felt that we must be her friends, and saw in us her only possible hope of escape. For that reason she had instantly thrown herself under our protection. This accounted for the singular confidence which she had manifested in us from the beginning.

Her wonderful story had so captivated our imaginations that for a long time after it was finished we could not recover from the spell. It was told over and over again from mouth to mouth, and repeated from ship to ship, everywhere exciting the utmost astonishment.

Destiny seemed to have sent us on this expedition into space for the purpose of clearing off mysteries that had long puzzled the minds of men. When on the moon we had unexpectedly to ourselves settled the question that had been debated from the beginning of astronomical history of the former habitability of that globe.

A Question Settled.

Now, on Mars, we had put to rest no less mysterious questions relating to the past history of our own planet. Adelung, as the Heidelberg Professor asserted, had named the Vale of Cashmere as the probable site of the Garden of Eden, and the place of origin of the human race, but later investigators had taken issue with this opinion, and the question where the Aryans originated upon the earth had long been one of the most puzzling that science presented.

This question seemed now to have been settled.

Aina had said that Mars had completed 5,000 circuits about the sun since her people were brought to it as captives. One circuit of Mars occupies 687 days. More than 9,000 years had therefore elapsed since the first invasion of the earth by the Martians.

Another great mystery—that of the origin of those gigantic and inexplicable monuments, the great pyramids and the Sphinx, on the banks of the Nile, had also apparently been solved by us, although these Egyptian wonders had been the furthest things from our thoughts when we set out for the planet Mars.

We had travelled more than thirty millions of miles in order to get answers to questions which could not be solved at home.

But from these speculations and retrospects we were recalled by the commander of the expedition.

Does Aina Hold the Secret?

"This is all very interesting and very romantic, gentlemen," he said, "but now let us get at the practical side of it. We have learned Aina's language and have heard her story. Let us next ascertain whether she cannot place in our hands some key which will place Mars at our mercy. Remember what we came here for, and remember that the earth expects every man of us to do his duty."

This Nelson-like summons again changed the current of our thoughts, and we instantly set to work to learn from Aina if Mars, like Achilles, had not some vulnerable point where a blow would be mortal.

Chapter XIV

It was a curious scene when the momentous interview which was to determine our fate and that of Mars began. Aina had been warned of what was coming. We in the flagship had all learned to speak her language with more or less ease, but it was deemed best that the Heidelberg Professor, assisted by one of his colleagues, should act as interpreter.

The girl, flushed with excitement of the novel situation, fully appreciating the importance of what was about to occur, and looking more charming than before, stood at one side of the principal apartment. Directly facing her were the interpreters, and the rest of us, all with ears intent and eyes focused upon Aina, stood in a double row behind them.

As heretofore, I am setting down her words translated into our own tongue, having taken only so much liberty as to connect the sentences into a stricter sequence than they had when falling from her lips in reply to the questions that were showered upon her.

She Has a Plan.

"You will never be victorious," she said, "if you attack them openly as you have been doing. They are too strong and too numerous. They are well prepared for such attacks, because they have had to resist them before."

Aina's Plan to Capture Mars.

Our beautiful captive tells us that it will be impossible for us to subdue the Martians in a hand-to-hand conflict, but reveals a plan to exterminate them which is gigantic in its scope and originality.

"They have waged war with the inhabitants of the asteroid Ceres, whose people are giants greater than themselves. Their enemies from Ceres have attacked them here. Hence these fortifications, with weapons pointing skyward, and the great air fleets which you have encountered."

"But there must be some point," said Mr. Edison, "where we can."

"Yes, yes," interrupted the girl quickly, "there is one blow you can deal them which they could not withstand."

"What is that?" eagerly inquired the commander.

"You can drown them out."

"How? With the canals?"

We Must Drown Them Out.

"Yes, I will explain to you. I have already told you, and, in fact, you must have seen it for yourselves, that there are almost no mountains on Mars. A very learned man of my race used to say that the reason was because Mars is so very old a world that the mountains it once had have been almost completely levelled, and the entire surface of the planet had become a great plain. There are depressions, however, most of which are occupied by the seas. The greater part of the land lies below the level of the oceans. In order at the same time to irrigate the soil and make it fruitful, and to protect themselves from overflows by the ocean breaking in upon them, the Martians have constructed the immense and innumerable canals which you see running in all directions over the continents."

"There is one period in the year, and that period has now arrived, when there is special danger of a great deluge. Most of the oceans of Mars lie in the southern hemisphere. When it is Summer in that hemisphere, the great masses of ice and snow collected around the south pole melt rapidly away."

"Yes, that is so," broke in one of our astronomers, who was listening attentively. "Many a time I have seen the vast snow fields around the southern pole of Mars completely disappear as the Summer sun rose high upon them."

"With the melting of these snows," continued Aina, "a rapid rise in the level of the water in the southern oceans occurs. On the side facing these oceans the continents of Mars are sufficiently elevated to prevent an overflow, but nearer the equator the level of the land sinks lower."

"With your telescopes you have no doubt noticed that there is a great bending sea connecting the oceans of the south with those of the north and running through the midst of the continents."

"Quite so," said the astronomer who had spoken before, "we call it the Syrtis Major."

"That long narrow sea," Aina went on, "forms a great channel through which the flood of waters caused by the melting of the southern polar snows flows swiftly toward the equator and then on toward the north until it reaches the sea basins which exist there. At that point it is rapidly turned into ice and snow, because, of course, while it is Summer in the southern hemisphere it is Winter in the northern."

Mars Will Be Ours.

"The Syrtis Major (I am giving our name to the channel of communication in place of that by which the girl called it) is like a great safety valve, which, by permitting the waters to flow northward, saves the continents from inundation."

"But when mid-Summer arrives, the snows around the pole having been completely melted away, the flood ceases and the water begins to recede. At this time, but for a device which the Martians have employed, the canals connected with the oceans would run dry, and the vegetation, left without moisture under the Summer sun, would quickly perish."

"To prevent this they have built a series of enormous gates extending completely across the Syrtis Major at its narrowest point (latitude 25 degrees south). These gates are all controlled by machinery collected at a single point on the shore of the strait. As soon as the flood in the Syrtis Major begins to recede, the gates are closed, and, the water being thus restrained, the irrigating canals are kept full long enough to mature the harvests."

"The clew! The clew at last!" exclaimed Mr. Edison. "That is the place where we shall nip them. If we can close those gates now at the moment of high tide we shall flood the country. Did you say," he continued, turning to Aina, "that the movement of the gates was all controlled from a single point?"

The Great Power House.

"Yes," said the girl. "There is a great building (power house) full of tremendous machinery which I once entered when my father was taken there by his master, and where I saw one Martian, by turning a little handle, cause the great line of gates, stretching a hundred miles across the sea, to slowly shut in, edge to edge, until the flow of the water toward the north had been stopped."

"How is the building protected?"

"So completely," replied Aina, "that my only fear is that you may not be able to reach it. On account of the danger from their enemies on Ceres, the Martians have fortified it strongly on all sides, and have even surrounded it and covered it overhead with a great electrical network, to touch which would be instant death."

"Ah," said Mr. Edison, "they have got an electric shield, have they? Well, I think we shall be able to manage that."

"Anyhow," he continued, "we have got to get into that power house, and we have got to close those gates, and we must not lose much time in making up our minds how it is to be done. Evidently this is our only chance. We have not force enough to contend in open battle with the Martians, but if we can flood them out, and thereby render the engines contained in their fortifications useless, perhaps we shall be able to deal with the airships, which will be all the means of defence that will then remain to them."

This idea commended itself to all the leaders of the expedition. It was determined to make a reconnaissance at once.

But it would not do for us to approach the planet too hastily, and we certainly could not think of landing upon it in broad daylight. Still, as long as we were yet at a considerable distance from Mars, we felt that we should be safe from observation, because so much time had elapsed while we were hidden behind Deimos that the Martians had undoubtedly concluded that we were no longer in existence.

So we boldly quitted the little satellite with our entire squadron and once more rapidly approached the red planet of war. This time it was to be a death grapple and our chances of victory still seemed good.

Ready for a Death Grapple.

As soon as we arrived so near the planet that there was danger of our being actually seen, we took pains to keep continually in the shadow of Mars, and the more surely to conceal our presence all lights upon the ships were extinguished. The precaution of the commander even went so far as to have the smooth metallic sides of the cars blackened over so that they should not reflect light, and thus become visible to the Martians as shining specks, moving suspiciously among the stars.

The precise location of the great power house on the shores of the Syrtis Major having been carefully ascertained, the squadron dropped down one night into the upper limits of the Martian atmosphere, directly over the gulf.

Then a consultation was called on the flagship and a plan of campaign was quickly devised.

It was deemed wise that the attempt should be made with a single electrical ship, but that the others should be kept hovering near, ready to respond on the instant to any signal for aid which might come from below. It was thought that, notwithstanding the wonderful defences, which, according to Aina's account surrounded the building, a small party would have a better chance of success than a large one.

Mr. Edison was certain that the electrical network which was described as covering the power house would not prove a serious obstruction to us, because by carefully sweeping the space where we intended to pass with the disintegrators before quitting the ship, the netting could be sufficiently cleared away to give us uninterrupted passage.

At first the intention was to have twenty men, each armed with two disintegrators (that being the largest number that one person could carry to advantage) descend from the electrical ship and make the venture. But, after further discussion, this number was reduced; first to a dozen, and finally, to only four. These four consisted of Mr. Edison, Colonel Smith, Mr. Sidney Phillips and myself.

Both by her own request and because we could not help feeling that her knowledge of the locality would be indispensable to us, Aina was also included in our party, but not, of course, as a fighting member of it.

It was about an hour after midnight when the ship in which we were to make the venture parted from the remainder of the squadron and dropped cautiously down. The blaze of electric lights running away in various directions indicated the lines of innumerable canals with habitations crowded along their banks, which came to a focus at a point on the continent of Aeria, westward from the Syrtis Major.

Destroying The Martians.

With Aina's Aid Our Warriors Prepare an Awful Revenge on the Enemy.

We stopped the electrical ship at an elevation of perhaps three hundred feet above the vast roof of a structure which Aina assured us was the building we were in search of.

Here we remained for a few minutes, cautiously reconnoitring. On that side of the power house which was opposite to the shore of the Syrtis Major there was a thick grove of trees, lighted beneath, as was apparent from the illumination which here and there streamed up through the cover of leaves, but, nevertheless, dark and gloomy above the tree tops.

"The electric network extends over the grove as well as over the building," said Aina.

This was lucky for us, because we wished to descend among the trees, and, by destroying part of the network over the tree tops, we could reach the shelter we desired and at the same time pass within the line of electric defences.

With increased caution, and almost holding our breath lest we should make some noise that might reach the ears of the sentinels beneath, we caused the car to settle gently down until we caught sight of a metallic net stretched in the air between us and the trees.

After our first encounter with the Martians on the asteroid, where, as I have related, some metal which was included in their dress resisted the action of the disintegrators, Mr. Edison had readjusted the range of vibrations covered by the instruments, and since then we had found nothing that did not yield to them. Consequently, we had no fear that the metal of the network would not be destroyed.

There was danger, however, of arousing attention by shattering holes through the tree tops. This could be avoided by first carefully ascertaining how far away the network was, and then with the adjustable mirrors attached to the disintegrators focusing the vibratory discharge at that distance.

Overcoming Their Precautions.

So successful were we that we opened a considerable gap in the network without doing any perceptible damage to the trees beneath.

The ship was cautiously lowered through the opening and brought to rest among the upper branches of one of the tallest trees. Colonel Smith, Mr. Phillips, Mr. Edison and myself at once clambered out upon a strong limb.

For a moment I feared our arrival had been betrayed on account of the altogether too noisy contest that arose between Colonel Smith and Mr. Phillips as to which of them should assist Aina. To settle the dispute I took charge of her myself.

At length we were all safely in the tree.

Then followed the still more dangerous undertaking of descending from this great height to the ground. Fortunately, the branches were very close together and they extended down within a short distance of the soil. So the actual difficulties of the descent were not very great after all. The one thing that we had particularly to bear in mind was the absolute necessity of making no noise.

At length the descent was successfully accomplished, and we all five stood together in the shadow at the foot of the great tree. The grove was so thick around that while there was an abundance of electric lights among the trees, their illumination did not fall upon us where we stood.

Peering cautiously through the vistas in various directions, we ascertained our location with respect to the wall of the building. Like all the structures that we had seen on Mars, it was composed of polished red metal.

Looking for an Entrance.

"Where is the entrance?" inquired Mr. Edison, in a whisper.

"Come softly this way, and look out for the sentinel," replied Aina.

Gripping our disintegrators firmly, and screwing up our courage, with noiseless steps we followed the girl among the shadows of the trees.

We had one very great advantage. The Martians had evidently placed so much confidence in the electric network which surrounded the power house that they never dreamed of enemies being able to penetrate it—at least, without giving warning of their coming.

But the hole which we had blown in this network with the disintegrators had been made noiselessly, and Mr. Edison believed, since no enemies had appeared, that our operations had not been betrayed by any automatic signal to watchers inside the building.

Consequently, we had every reason to think that we now stood within the line of defence, in which they reposed the greatest confidence, without their having the least suspicion of our presence.

Aina assured us that on the occasion of her former visit to the power house there had been but two sentinels on guard at the entrance. At the inner end of a long passage leading to the interior, she said, there were two more. Besides these there were three or four Martian engineers watching the machinery in the interior of the building. A number of air ships were supposed to be on guard around the structure, but possibly their vigilance had been relaxed, because not long ago the Martians had sent an expedition against Ceres which had been so successful that the power of that planet to make an attack upon Mars had for the present been destroyed.

Supposing us to have been annihilated in the recent battle among the clouds, they would have no fear or cause for vigilance on our account.

The entrance to the great structure was low—at least, when measured by the stature of the Martians. Evidently the intention was that only one person at a time should find room to pass through it.

Drawing cautiously near, we discerned the outlines of two gigantic forms, standing in the darkness, one on either side of the door. Colonel Smith whispered to me:

The Disintegrator Again.

"If you will take the fellow on the right, I will attend to the other one."

Adjusting our aim as carefully as was possible in the gloom, Colonel Smith and I simultaneously discharged our disintegrators, sweeping them rapidly up and down in the manner which had become familiar to us when endeavoring to destroy one of the gigantic Martians with a single stroke. And so successful were we that the two sentinels disappeared as if they had been ghosts of the night.

Instantly we all hurried forward and entered the door. Before us extended a long, straight passage, brightly illuminated by a number of electric candles. Its polished sides gleamed with blood-red reflections, and the gallery terminated, at a distance of two or three hundred feet, with an opening into a large chamber beyond, on the further side of which we could see part of a gigantic and complicated mass of machinery.

Making as little noise as possible, we pushed ahead along the passage, but when we had arrived within a distance of a dozen paces from the inner end, we stopped, and Colonel Smith, getting down upon his knees, crept forward until he had reached the inner end of the passage. There he peered cautiously around the edge into the chamber, and, turning his head a moment later, beckoned us to come forward. We crept to his side, and, looking out into the vast apartment, could perceive no enemies.

What had become of the sentinels supposed to stand at the inner end of the passage we could not imagine. At any rate, they were not at their posts.

In the Great Power House.

The chamber was an immense square room at least a hundred feet in height and 400 feet on a side, and almost filling the wall opposite to us was an intricate display of machinery, wheels, levers, rods and polished plates. This we had no doubt was one end of the great engine which opened and shut the great gates that could dam an ocean.

"There is no one in sight," said Colonel Smith.

"Then we must act quickly," said Mr. Edison.

"Where," he said, turning to Aina, "is the handle by turning which you saw the Martian close the gates?"

Aina looked about in bewilderment. The mechanism before us was so complicated that even an expert mechanician would have been excusable for finding himself unable to understand it. There were scores of knobs and handles, all glistening in the electric light, any one of which, so far as the uninstructed could tell, might have been the master key that controlled the whole complex apparatus.

The Magic Lever!

"Quick," said Mr. Edison, "where is it?"

The girl in her confusion ran this way and that, gazing hopelessly upon the machinery, but evidently utterly unable to help us.

To remain here inactive was not merely to invite destruction for ourselves, but was sure to bring certain failure upon the purpose of the expedition. All of us began instantly to look about in search of the proper handle, seizing every crank and wheel in sight and striving to turn it.

"Stop that!" shouted Mr. Edison, "you may set the whole thing wrong. Don't touch anything until we have found the right lever."

But to find that seemed to most of us now utterly beyond the power of man.

It was at this critical moment that the wonderful depth and reach of Mr. Edison's mechanical genius displayed itself. He stepped back, ran his eye quickly over the whole immense mass of wheels, handles, bolts, bars and levers, paused for an instant, as if making up his mind, then said decidedly, "There it is," and, stepping quickly forward, selected a small wheel amid a dozen others, all furnished at the circumference with handles like those of a pilot's wheel, and, giving it a quick wrench, turned it half way around.

Surprised by the Enemy.

At this instant, a startling shout fell upon our ears. There was a thunderous clatter behind us, and, turning, we saw three gigantic Martians rushing forward.

Chapter XV

"Sweep them! Sweep them!" cried Colonel Smith, as he brought his disintegrator to bear. Mr. Phillips and I instantly followed his example, and thus we swept the Martians into eternity, while Mr. Edison coolly continued his manipulations of the wheel.

The effect of what he was doing became apparent in less than half a minute. A shiver ran through the mass of machinery and shook the entire building.

"Look! look!" cried Sidney Phillips, who had stepped a little apart from the others.

The Grand Canal.

We all ran to his side and found ourselves in front of a great window which opened through the side of the engine, giving a view of what lay in front of it. There, gleaming in the electric lights, we saw the Syrtis Major, its waters washing high against the walls of the vast power house. Running directly out from the shore, there was an immense metallic gate at least 400 yards in length and rising 300 feet above the present level of the water.

The Grand Rush of Waters.

We all ran to his side and found ourselves in front of a great window. There, gleaming in the electric light, we saw the Syrtis Major, its waters washing high against the walls of the vast power house!

This great gate was slowly swinging upon an invisible hinge in such a manner that in a few minutes it would evidently stand across the current of the Syrtis Major at right angles.

Beyond was a second gate, which was moving in the same manner. Further on was a third gate, and then another, and another, as far as the eye could reach, evidently extending in an unbroken series completely across the great strait.

As the gates, with accelerated motion when the current caught them, clanged together, we beheld a spectacle that almost stopped the beating of our hearts.

A Great Rush of Waters.

The great Syrtis seemed to gather itself for a moment, and then it leaped upon the obstruction and hurled its waters into one vast foaming geyser that seemed to shoot a thousand feet skyward.

But the metal gates withstood the shock, though buried from our sight in the seething white mass, and the baffled waters instantly swirled round in ten thousand gigantic eddies, rising to the level of our window and beginning to inundate the power house before we fairly comprehended our peril.

"We have done the work," said Mr. Edison, smiling grimly. "Now we had better get out of this before the flood bursts upon us."

The warning came none too soon. It was necessary to act upon it at once if we would save our lives. Even before we could reach the entrance to the long passage through which we had come into the great engine room, the water had risen half way to our knees. Colonel Smith, catching Aina under his arm, led the way. The roar of the maddened torrent behind deafened us.

As we ran through the passage, the water followed us, with a wicked swishing sound, and within five seconds it was above our knees; in ten seconds up to our waists.

The great danger now was that we should be swept from our feet, and once down in that torrent there would have been little chance of our ever getting our heads above its level. Supporting ourselves as best we could with the aid of the walls, we partly ran, and were partly swept along, until, when we reached the outer end of the passage and emerged into the open air, the flood was swirling about our shoulders.

Escaping the Water.

Here there was an opportunity to clutch some of the ornamental work surrounding the doorway, and thus we managed to stay our mad progress, and gradually to work out of the current until we found that the water, having now an abundance of room to spread, had fallen again as low as our knees.

But suddenly we heard the thunder of the banks tumbling behind us, and to the right and left, and the savage growl of the released water as it sprang through the breaches.

To my dying day, I think, I shall not forget the sight of a great fluid column that burst through the dyke at the edge of the grove of trees, and, by the tremendous impetus of its rush, seemed turned into a solid thing.

Like an enormous ram, it plowed the soil to a depth of twenty feet, uprooting acres of the immense trees like stubble turned over by the plowshare.

The uproar was so awful that for an instant the coolest of us lost our self-control. Yet we knew that we had not the fraction of a second to waste. The breaking of the banks had caused the water again rapidly to rise about us. In a little while it was once more as high as our waists.

In the excitement and confusion, deafened by the noise and blinded by the flying foam, we were in danger of becoming separated in the flood. We no longer knew certainly in what direction was the tree by whose aid we had ascended from the electrical ship. We pushed first one way and then another, staggering through the rushing waters in search of it. Finally we succeeded in locating it, and with all our strength hurried toward it.

Then there came a noise as if the globe of Mars had been split asunder, and another great head of water hurled itself down upon the soil before us, and, without taking time to spread, bored a vast cavity in the ground, and scooped out the whole of the grove before our eyes as easily as a gardener lifts a sod with his spade.

Are We, Too, Destroyed?

Our last hope was gone. For a moment the level of the water around us sank again, as it poured into the immense excavation where the grove had stood, but in an instant it was reinforced from all sides and began once more rapidly to rise.

We gave ourselves up for lost, and, indeed, there did not seem any possible hope of salvation.

Even in the extremity I saw Colonel Smith lifting the form of Aina, who had fainted, above the surface of the surging water, while Sidney Phillips stood by his side and aided him in supporting the unconscious girl.

"We stayed a little too long," was the only sound I heard from Mr. Edison.

The huge bulk of the power house partially protected us against the force of the current, and the water spun around us in great eddies. These swept us this way and that, but yet we managed to cling together, determined not to be separated in death if we could avoid it.

Suddenly a cry rang out directly above our heads:

"Jump for your lives, and be quick!"

At the same instant the ends of several ropes splashed into the water.

We glanced upward, and there, within three or four yards of our heads, hung the electrical ship, which we had left moored at the top of the tree.

Tom, the expert electrician from Mr. Edison's shop, who had remained in charge of the ship, had never once dreamed of such a thing as deserting us. The moment he saw the water bursting over the dam, and evidently flooding the building which we had entered, he cast off his moorings, as we subsequently learned, and hovered over the entrance to the power house, getting as low down as possible and keeping a sharp watch for us.

But most of the electric lights in the vicinity had been carried down by the first rush of water, and in the darkness he did not see us when we emerged from the entrance. It was only after the sweeping away of the grove of trees had allowed a flood of light to stream upon the scene from a cluster of electric lamps on a distant portion of the bank on the Syrtis that had not yet given way that he caught sight of us.

Mars Is Ruined!

Immediately he began to shout to attract our attention, but in the awful uproar we could not hear him. Getting together all the ropes that he could lay his hands on, he steered the ship to a point directly over us, and then dropped down within a few yards of the boiling flood.

Now as he hung over our heads, and saw the water up to our very necks and still swiftly rising, he shouted again:

"Catch hold, for God's sake!"

The three men who were with him in the ship seconded his cries.

But by the time we had fairly grasped the ropes, so rapidly was the flood rising, we were already afloat. With the assistance of Tom and his men we were rapidly drawn up, and immediately Tom reversed the electric polarity, and the ship began to rise.

At that same instant, with a crash that shivered the air, the immense metallic power house gave way and was swept tumbling, like a hill torn loose from its base, over the very spot where a moment before we had stood. One second's hesitation on the part of Tom, and the electrical ship would have been battered into a shapeless wad of metal by the careening mass.

The Deluge On Mars.

How the Martians Met Their Doom Through Aina's Plans.

When we had attained a considerable height, so that we could see to a great distance on either side, the spectacle became even more fearful than it was when we were close to the surface.

On all sides banks and dykes were going down; trees were being uprooted; buildings were tumbling, and the ocean was achieving that victory over the land which had long been its due, but which the ingenuity of the inhabitants of Mars had postponed for ages.

Far away we could see the front of the advancing wave crested with foam that sparkled in the electric lights, and as it swept on it changed the entire aspect of the planet—in front of it all life, behind it all death.

Eastward our view extended across the Syrtis Major toward the land of Libya and the region of Isidis. On that side also the dykes were giving way under the tremendous pressure, and the floods were rushing toward the sunrise, which had just begun to streak the eastern sky.

The continents that were being overwhelmed on the western side of the Syrtis were Meroe, Aeria, Arabia, Edom and Eden.

The water beneath us continually deepened. The current from the melting snows around the southern pole was at its strongest, and one could hardly have believed that any obstruction put in its path would have been able to arrest it and turn it into these two all-swallowing deluges, sweeping east and west. But, as we now perceived, the level of the land over a large part of its surface was hundreds of feet below the ocean, so that the latter, when once the barriers were broken, rushed into depressions that yawned to receive it.

Waiting for the Flood.

The point where we had dealt our blow was far removed from the great capital of Mars, around the Lake of the Sun, and we knew that we should have to wait for the floods to reach that point before the desired effect could be produced. By the nearest way, the water had at least 5,000 miles to travel. We estimated that its speed where we hung above it was as much as a hundred miles an hour. Even if that speed were maintained, more than two days and nights would be required for the floods to reach the Lake of the Sun.

But as the water rushed on it would break the banks of all the canals intersecting the country, and these, being also elevated above the surface, would add the impetus of their escaping waters to hasten the advance of the flood. We calculated, therefore, that about two days would suffice to place the planet at our mercy.

Half way from the Syrtis Major to the Lake of the Sun another great connecting link between the Southern and Northern ocean basins, called on our maps of Mars the Indus, existed, and through this channel we knew that another great current must be setting from the south toward the north. The flood that we had started would reach and break the banks of the Indus within one day.

Flooding Hundreds of Canals.

The flood travelling in the other direction, towards the east, would have considerably further to go before reaching the neighborhood of the Lake of the Sun. It, too, would involve hundreds of great canals as it advanced and would come plunging upon the Lake of the Sun and its surrounding forts and cities, probably about half a day later than the arrival of the deluge that travelled towards the west.

Now that we had let the awful destroyer loose we almost shrank from the thought of the consequences which we had produced. How many millions would perish as the result of our deed we could not even guess. Many of the victims, so far as we knew, might be entirely innocent of enmity toward us, or of the evil which had been done to our native planet. But this was a case in which the good—if they existed—must suffer with the bad on account of the wicked deeds of the latter.

I have already remarked that the continents of Mars were higher on their northern and southern borders where they faced the great oceans. These natural barriers bore to the main mass of the land somewhat the relation of the edge of a shallow dish to its bottom. Their rise on the land side was too gradual to give them the appearance of hills, but on the side toward the sea they broke down in steep banks and cliffs several hundred feet in height. We guessed that it would be in the direction of these elevations that the inhabitants would flee, and those who had timely warning might thus be able to escape in case the flood did not—as it seemed possible it might in its first mad rush—overtop the highest elevations on Mars.

A Dreadful Scene.

As day broke and the sun slowly rose upon the dreadful scene beneath us, we began to catch sight of some of the fleeing inhabitants. We had shifted the position of the fleet toward the south, and were now suspended above the southeastern corner of Aeria. Here a high bank of reddish rock confronted the sea, whose waters ran lashing and roaring along the bluffs to supply the rapid draught produced by the emptying of the Syrtis Major. Along the shore there was a narrow line of land, hundreds of miles in length, but less than a quarter of a mile broad, which still rose slightly above the surface of the water, and this land of refuge was absolutely packed with the monstrous inhabitants of the planet who had fled hither on the first warning that the water was coming.

In some places it was so crowded that the later comers could not find standing ground on dry land, but were continually slipping back and falling into the water. It was an awful sight to look at them. It reminded me of pictures that I had seen of the deluge in the days of Noah, when the waters had risen to the mountain tops, and men, women and children were fighting for a foothold upon the last dry spots that the earth contained.

The Martians Penned in by the Flood.

This land of refuge was absolutely packed with the monstrous inhabitants of the planet, who had fled hither on the first warning that the water was coming.

We were all moved by a desire to help our enemies, for we were overwhelmed with feelings of pity and remorse, but to aid them was now utterly beyond our power. The mighty floods were out, and the end was in the hands of God.

Fortunately, we had little time for these thoughts, because no sooner had the day begun to dawn around us than the airships of the Martians appeared. Evidently the people in them were dazed by the disaster and uncertain what to do. It is doubtful whether at first they comprehended the fact that we were the agents who had produced the cataclysm.

The Flocking of the Airships.

But as the morning advanced the airships came flocking in greater and greater numbers from every direction, many swooping down close to the flood in order to rescue those who were drowning. Hundreds gathered along the slip of land which was crowded as I have described, with refugees, while other hundreds rapidly assembled about us, evidently preparing for an attack.

We had learned in our previous contests with the airships of the Martians that our electrical ships had a great advantage over them, not merely in rapidity and facility of movement, but in the fact that our disintegrators could sweep in every direction, while it was only with much difficulty that the Martian airships could discharge their electrical strokes at an enemy poised directly above their heads.

Accordingly, orders were instantly flashed to all the squadron to rise vertically to an elevation so great that the rarity of the atmosphere would prevent the airships from attaining the same level.

Outwitting the Enemy.

This manoeuvre was executed so quickly that the Martians were unable to deal us a blow before we were poised above them in such a position that they could not easily reach us. Still they did not mean to give up the conflict.

Presently we saw one of the largest of their ships manoeuvring in a very peculiar manner, the purpose of which we did not at first comprehend. Its forward portion commenced slowly to rise, until it pointed upward like the nose of a fish approaching the surface of the water. The moment it was in this position, an electrical bolt was darted from its prow, and one of our ships received a shock which, although it did not prove fatal to the vessel itself, killed two or three men aboard it, disarranged its apparatus, and rendered it for the time being useless.

"Ah, that's their trick, is it?" said Mr. Edison. "We must look out for that. Whenever you see one of the airships beginning to stick its nose up after that fashion blaze away at it."

An order to this effect was transmitted throughout the squadron. At the same time several of the most powerful disintegrators were directed upon the ship which had executed the stratagem and, reduced to a wreck, it dropped, whirling like a broken kite until it fell into the flood beneath.

A Thousand Martian Ships.

Still the Martians' ships came flocking in ever greater numbers from all directions. They made desperate attempts to attain the level at which we hung above them. This was impossible, but many, getting an impetus by a swift run in the denser portion of the atmosphere beneath, succeeded in rising so high that they could discharge their electric artillery with considerable effect. Others, with more or less success, repeated the manoeuvre of the ship which had first attacked us, and thus the battle became gradually more general and more fierce, until, in the course of an hour or two, our squadron found itself engaged with probably a thousand airships, which blazed with incessant lightning strokes, and were able, all too frequently, to do us serious damage.

But on our part the battle was waged with a cool determination and a consciousness of insuperable advantage which boded ill for the enemy. Only three or four of our sixty electrical ships were seriously damaged, while the work of the disintegrators upon the crowded fleet that floated beneath us was terrible to look upon.

They Battle on in Earnest.

Our strokes fell thick and fast on all sides. It was like firing into a flock of birds that could not get away. Notwithstanding all their efforts they were practically at our mercy. Shattered into unrecognizable fragments, hundreds of the airships continually dropped from their great height to be swallowed up in the boiling waters.

Yet they were game to the last. They made every effort to get at us, and in their frenzy they seemed to discharge their bolts without much regard to whether friends or foes were injured. Our eyes were nearly blinded by the ceaseless glare beneath us, and the uproar was indescribable.

At length, after this fearful contest had lasted for at least three hours, it became evident that the strength of the enemy was rapidly weakening. Nearly the whole of their immense fleet of airships had been destroyed, or so far damaged that they were barely able to float. Just so long, however, as they showed signs of resistance we continued to pour our merciless fire upon them, and the signal to cease was not given until the airships which had escaped serious damage began to flee in every direction.

Victory Is Ours!

"Thank God, the thing is over," said Mr. Edison. "We have got the victory at last, but how we shall make use of it is something that at present I do not see."

"But will they not renew the attack," asked someone.

"I do not think they can," was the reply. "We have destroyed the very flower of their fleet."

"And better than that," said Colonel Smith, "we have destroyed their elan; we have made them afraid. Their discipline is gone."

But this was only the beginning of our victory. The floods below were achieving a still greater triumph, and now that we had conquered the airships we dropped within a few hundred feet of the surface of the water and then turned our faces westward in order to follow the advance of the deluge and see whether, as we had hoped, it would overwhelm our enemies in the very centre of their power.

The Flood Advances.

In a little while we had overtaken the front wave, which was still devouring everything. We saw it bursting the banks of the canals, sweeping away forests of gigantic trees, and swallowing cities and villages, leaving nothing but a broad expanse of swirling and eddying waters, which, in consequence of the prevailing red hue of the vegetation and the soil, looked, as shuddering we gazed down upon it, like an ocean of blood flecked with foam and steaming with the escaping life of the planet from whose veins it gushed.

As we skirted the southern borders of the continent the same dreadful scenes which we had beheld on the coast of Aeria presented themselves. Crowds of refugees thronged the high border of the land and struggled with one another for a foothold against the continually rising flood.

Watching the Destruction.

We saw, too, flitting in every direction, but rapidly fleeing before our approach, many airships, evidently crowded with Martians, but not armed either for offence or defence. These, of course, we did not disturb, for merciless as our proceedings seemed even to ourselves, we had no intention of making war upon the innocent, or upon those who had no means to resist. What we had done it had seemed to us necessary to do, but henceforth we were resolved to take no more lives if it could be avoided.

Thus, during the remainder of that day, all of the following night and all of the next day, we continued upon the heels of the advancing flood.

Chapter XVI

The second night we could perceive ahead of us the electric lights covering the land of Thaumasia, in the midst of which lay the Lake of the Sun. The flood would be upon it by daybreak, and, assuming that the demoralization produced by the news of the coming of the waters, which we were aware had hours before been flashed to the capital of Mars, would prevent the Martians from effectively manning their forts, we thought it safe to hasten on with the flagship, and one or two others, in advance of the water, and to hover over the Lake of the Sun in the darkness, in order that we might watch the deluge perform its awful work in the morning.

The Giant Woman Drowned.

She, Like the Rest, a Prey to the Devouring Flood of the Canals.

Thaumasia, as I have before remarked, was a broad, oval land, about 1,800 miles across, having the Lake of the Sun exactly in its centre. From this lake, which was four or five hundred miles in diameter, and circular in outline, many canals radiated, as straight as the spokes of a wheel, in every direction, and connected it with the surrounding seas.

Like all the other Martian continents, Thaumasia lay below the level of the sea, except toward the south, where it fronted the ocean.

Completely surrounding the lake was a great ring of cities constituting the capital of Mars. Here the genius of the Martians had displayed itself to the full. The surrounding country was irrigated until it fairly bloomed with gigantic vegetation and flowers; the canals were carefully regulated with locks so that the supply of water was under complete control; the display of magnificent metallic buildings of all kinds and sizes produced a most dazzling effect, and the protection against enemies afforded by the innumerable fortifications surrounding the ringed city, and guarding the neighboring lands, seemed complete.

Waiting for the Flood.

Suspended at a height of perhaps two miles from the surface, near the southern edge of the lake, we waited for the oncoming flood. With the dawn of day we began to perceive more clearly the effects which the news of the drowning of the planet had produced. It was evident that many of the inhabitants of the cities had already fled. Airships on which the fugitives hung as thick as swarms of bees were seen, elevated but a short distance above the ground, and making their way rapidly toward the south.

The Martians knew that their only hope of escape lay in reaching the high southern border of the land before the floods were upon them. But they must have known also that that narrow beach would not suffice to contain one in ten of those who sought refuge there. The density of the population around the Lake of the Sun seemed to us incredible. Again our hearts sank within us at the sight of the fearful destruction of life for which we were responsible. Yet we comforted ourselves with the reflection that it was unavoidable. As Colonel Smith put it:

"You couldn't trust these coyotes. The only thing to do was to drown them out. I am sorry for them, but I guess there will be as many left as will be good for us, anyhow."

The Crest of the Waters.

We had not long to wait for the flood. As the dawn began to streak the east we saw its awful crest moving out of the darkness, bursting across the canals and plowing its way in the direction of the crowded shores of the Lake of the Sun. The supply of water behind that great wave seemed inexhaustible. Five thousand miles it had travelled, and yet its power was as great as when it started from the Syrtis Major.

We caught sight of the oncoming water before it was visible to the Martians beneath us. But while it was yet many miles away, the roar of it reached them, and then arose a chorus of terrified cries, the effect of which, coming to our ears out of the half gloom of the morning, was most uncanny and horrible. Thousands upon thousands of the Martians still remained here to become the victims of the deluge. Some, perhaps, had doubted the truth of the reports that the banks were down and the floods were out; others, for one reason or another had been unable to get away; others, like the inhabitants of Pompeii, had lingered too long, or had returned after beginning their flight to secure abandoned treasures, and now it was too late to get away.

Engulfing the City.

With a roar that shook the planet the white wall rushed upon the great city beneath our feet, and in an instant it had been engulfed. On went the flood, swallowing up the Lake of the Sun itself, and in a little while, as far as our eyes could range, the land of Thaumasia had been turned into a raging sea.

We now turned our ships toward the southern border of the land, following the direction of the airships carrying the fugitives, a few of which were still navigating the atmosphere a mile beneath us. In their excitement and terror the Martians paid little attention to us, although, as the morning brightened, they must have been aware of our presence over their heads. But, apparently, they no longer thought of resistance; their only object was escape from the immediate and appalling danger.

When we had progressed to a point about half way from the Lake of the Sun to the border of the sea, having dropped down within a few hundred feet of the surface, there suddenly appeared, in the midst of the raging waters, a sight so remarkable that at first I rubbed my eyes in astonishment, not crediting their report of what they beheld.

A Woman Forty Feet High!

Standing on the apex of a sandy elevation, which still rose a few feet above the gathering flood, was the figure of a woman, as perfect in form and in classic beauty of feature as the Venus of Milo—a magnified human being not less than forty feet in height!

But for her swaying and the wild motions of her arms, we should have mistaken her for a marble statue.

Aina, who happened to be looking, instantly exclaimed:

"It is the woman from Ceres. She was taken prisoner by the Martians during their last invasion of that world, and since then has been a slave in the palace of the Emperor."

Overtaken by the Flood.

Apparently her great stature had enabled her to escape, while her masters had been drowned. She had fled like the others, toward the south, but being finally surrounded by the rising waters, had taken refuge on the hillock of sand, where we saw her. This was fast giving way under the assault of the waves, and even while we watched the water rose to her knees.

"Drop lower," was the order of the electrical steersman of the flagship, and as quickly as possible we approached the place where the towering figure stood.

She had realized the hopelessness of her situation, and quickly ceased those appalling and despairing gestures, which at first served to convince us that it was indeed a living being on whom we were looking.

Save the Woman from Ceres!

There she stood, with a light, white garment thrown about her, erect, half-defiant, half yielding to her fear, more graceful than any Greek statue, her arms outstretched, yet motionless, and her eyes upcast, as if praying to her God to protect her. Her hair, which shone like gold in the increasing light of day, streamed over her shoulders, and her great eyes were astare between terror and supplication. So wildly beautiful a sight not one of us had ever beheld. For a moment sympathy was absorbed in admiration. Then:

"Save her! Save her!" was the cry that arose throughout the ship.

Ropes were instantly thrown out, and one or two men prepared to let themselves down in order better to aid her.

But when we were almost within reach, and so close that we could see the very expression of her eyes, which appeared to take no note of us, but to be fixed, with a far-away look upon something beyond human ken, suddenly the undermined bank on which she stood gave way, the blood-red flood swirled in from right to left, and then:

> "The waters closed above her face
> With many a ring."

The Beautiful Cerean Giantess Drowned in the Flood.

Standing on the apex of a sandy elevation, which still rose a few feet above the gathering flood, was the figure of a woman, as perfect in form and in classic beauty of feature as the Venus of Milo—a magnified human being not less than forty feet in height.

She, Like the Rest, Is Gone.

"If but for that woman's sake, I am sorry we drowned the planet," exclaimed Sidney Phillips. But a moment afterward I saw that he regretted what he had said, for Aina's eyes were fixed upon him. Perhaps, however, she did not understand his remark, and perhaps if she did it gave her no offence.

After this episode we pursued our way rapidly until we arrived at the shore of the Southern Ocean. There, as we had expected, was to be seen a narrow strip of land with the ocean on one side and the raging flood seeking to destroy it on the other. In some places it had been already broken through, so that the ocean was flowing in to assist in the drowning of Thaumasia.

But some parts of the coast were evidently so elevated that no matter how high the flood might rise it would not completely cover them. Here the fugitives had gathered in dense throngs and above them hovered most of the airships, loaded down with others who were unable to find room upon the dry land.

The Martians Not Discouraged.

On one of the loftiest and broadest of these elevations we noticed indications of military order in the alignment of the crowds and the shore all around was guarded by gigantic pickets, who mercilessly shoved back into the flood all the later comers, and thus prevented too great crowding upon the land. In the centre of this elevation rose a palatial structure of red metal which Aina informed us was one of the residences of the Emperor, and we concluded that the monarch himself was now present there.

The absence of any signs of resistance on the part of the airships, and the complete drowning of all of the formidable fortifications on the surface of the planet, convinced us that all we now had to do in order to complete our conquest was to get possession of the person of the chief ruler.

The fleet was, accordingly, concentrated, and we rapidly approached the great Martian palace. As we came down within a hundred feet of them and boldly made our way among their airships, which retreated at our approach, the Martians gazed at us with mingled fear and astonishment.

We were their conquerors and they knew it. We were coming to demand their surrender, and they evidently understood that also. As we approached the palace signals were made from it with brilliant colored banners which Aina informed us were intended as a token of truce.

"We shall have to go down and have a confab with them, I suppose," said Mr. Edison. "We can't kill them off now that they are helpless, but we must manage somehow to make them understand that unconditional surrender is their only chance."

A Parley with the Enemy.

"Let us take Aina with us," I suggested, "and since she can speak the language of the Martians we shall probably have no difficulty in arriving at an understanding."

Accordingly the flagship was carefully brought further down in front of the entrance to the palace, which had been kept clear by the Martian guards, and while the remainder of the squadron assembled within a few feet directly over our heads with the disintegrators turned upon the palace and the crowd below. Mr.

Edison and myself, accompanied by Aina, stepped out upon the ground.

There was a forward movement in the immense crowd, but the guards sternly kept everybody back. A party of a dozen giants, preceded by one who seemed to be their commander, gorgeously attired in jewelled garments, advanced from the entrance of the palace to meet us. Aina addressed a few words to the leader, who replied sternly, and then, beckoning us to follow, retraced his steps into the palace.

Notwithstanding our confidence that all resistance had ceased, we did not deem it wise actually to venture into the lion's den without having taken every precaution against a surprise. Accordingly, before following the Martian into the palace, we had twenty of the electrical ships moored around it in such a position that they commanded not only the entrance but all of the principal windows, and then a party of forty picked men, each doubly armed with powerful disintegrators, were selected to attend us into the building. This party was placed under the command of Colonel Smith, and Sidney Phillips insisted on being a member of it.

A Nearer Sight of the Martians.

In the meantime the Martian with his attendants who had first invited us to enter, finding that we did not follow him, had returned to the front of the palace. He saw the disposition that we had made of our forces, and instantly comprehended its significance, for his manner changed somewhat, and he seemed more desirous than before to conciliate us.

When he again beckoned us to enter, we unhesitatingly followed him, and, passing through the magnificent entrance, found ourselves in a vast ante-chamber, adorned after the manner of the Martians in the most expensive manner. Thence we passed into a great circular apartment, with a dome painted in imitation of the sky, and so lofty that to our eyes it seemed like the firmament itself. Here we found ourselves approaching an elevated throne situated in the centre of the apartment, while long rows of brilliantly armored guards flanked us on either side, and, grouped around the throne, some standing and others reclining upon the flights of steps which appeared to be of solid gold, was an array of Martian woman, beautifully and becomingly attired, all of whom greatly astonished us by the singular charm of their faces and bearing, so different from the aspect of most of the Martians, whom we had already encountered.

The Martians' Beautiful Women.

Despite their stature—for these women averaged twelve or thirteen feet in height—the beauty of their complexions—of a dark, olive tint—was no less brilliant than that of the women of Italy or Spain.

At the top of the steps on a magnificent golden throne, sat the Emperor himself. There are some busts of Caracalla which I have seen that are almost as ugly as the face of the Martian ruler. He was of gigantic stature, larger than the majority of his subjects, and as near as I could judge must have been between fifteen and sixteen feet in height.

As I looked at him I understood a remark which had been made by Aina to the effect that the Martians were not all alike, and that the peculiarities of their minds were imprinted on their faces and expressed in their forms in a very wonderful, and sometimes terrible manner.

I had also learned from her that Mars was under a military government, and that the military class had absolute control of the planet. I was somewhat startled, then, in looking at the head and centre of the great military system of Mars, to find in his appearance a striking confirmation of the speculations of our terrestrial phrenologists. His broad, mis-shapen head bulged in those parts where they had placed the so-called organs of combativeness, destructiveness, etc.

Something Learned About Them.

Plainly, this was an effect of his training and education. His very brain had become a military engine; and the aspect of his face, the pitiless lines of his mouth and chin, the evil glare of his eyes, the attitude and carriage of his muscular body, all tended to complete the warlike ensemble.

He was magnificently dressed in some vesture that had the lustre of a polished plate of gold, with the suppleness of velvet. As we approached he fixed his immense, deep-set eyes sternly upon our faces.

The contrast between his truly terrible countenance and the Eve-like features of the women who surrounded his throne was as great as if Satan after his fall had here re-enthroned himself in the midst of angels.

Mr. Edison, Colonel Smith, Sidney Phillips, Aina and myself advanced at the head of the procession, our guard following in close order behind us. It had been evident from the moment that we entered the palace that Aina was regarded with aversion by all of the Martians. Even the women about the throne gazed scowlingly at her as we drew near. Apparently, the bitterness of feeling which had led to the awful massacre of all her race had not yet vanished. And, indeed, since the fact that she remained alive could have been known only to the Martian who had abducted her and to his immediate companions, her reappearance with us must have been a great surprise to all those who now looked upon her.

The Enemy Vanquished.

The Martians Succumb at Last, and Are at Our Mercy.

It was clear to me that the feeling aroused by her appearance was every moment becoming more intense. Still, the thought of a violent outbreak did not occur to me, because our recent triumph had seemed so complete that I believed the Martians would be awed by our presence, and would not undertake actually to injure the girl.

I think we all had the same impression, but as the event proved, we were mistaken.

Suddenly one of the gigantic guards, as if actuated by a fit of ungovernable hatred, lifted his foot and kicked Aina. With a loud shriek, she fell to the floor.

Aina Attacked by a Martian.

The blow was so unexpected that for a second we all remained riveted to the spot. Then I saw Colonel Smith's face turn livid, and at the same instant heard the whirr of his disintegrator, while Sidney Phillips, forgetting the deadly instrument that he carried in his hand, sprung madly toward the brute who had kicked Aina, as if he intended to throttle him, colossus as he was.

But Colonel Smith's aim, though instantaneously taken, as he had been accustomed to shoot on the plains, was true, and Phillips, plunging madly forward, seemed wreathed in a faint blue mist—all that the disintegrator had left of the gigantic Martian.

Swift Vengeance.

Who could adequately describe the scene that followed?

I remember that the Martian Emperor sprang to his feet, looking tenfold more terrible than before. I remember that there instantly burst from the line of guards on either side crinkling beams of death-fire that seemed to sear the eyeballs. I saw a half a dozen of our men fall in heaps of ashes, and even at that terrible moment I had time to wonder that a single one of us remained alive.

Rather by instinct than in consequence of any order given, we formed ourselves in a hollow square, with Aina lying apparently lifeless in the centre, and then with gritted teeth we did our work.

The lines of guards melted before the disintegrators like rows of snow men before a licking flame.

A Terrible Battle.

The discharge of the lightning engines in the hands of the Martians in that confined space made an uproar so tremendous that it seemed to pass the bounds of human sense.

More of our men fell before their awful fire, and for the second time since our arrival on this dreadful planet of war our annihilation seemed inevitable.

But in a moment the whole scene changed. Suddenly there was a discharge into the room which I knew came from one of the disintegrators of the electrical ships. It swept through the crowded throng like a destroying blast. Instantly from another side swished a second discharge, no less destructive, and this was quickly followed by a third. Our ships were firing through the windows.

The Power of the Disintegrator.

Almost at the same moment I saw the flagship, which had been moored in the air close to the entrance and floating only three or four feet above the ground, pushing its way through the gigantic doorway from the ante-room, with its great disintegrators pointed upon the crowd like the muzzles of a cruiser's guns.

And now the Martians saw that the contest was hopeless for them, and their mad struggle to get out of the range of the disintegrators and to escape from the death chamber was more appalling to look upon than anything that had yet occurred.

It was a panic of giants. They trod one another under foot; they yelled and screamed in their terror; they tore each other with their clawlike fingers. They no longer thought of resistance. The battle spirit had been blown out of them by a breath of terror that shivered their marrow.

No Pity for Our Foes.

Still the pitiless disintegrators played upon them until Mr. Edison, making himself heard, now that the thunder of their engines had ceased to reverberate through the chamber, commanded that our fire should cease.

The Remorseless Slaughter of the Martians.

Suddenly there was a discharge into the room which I knew came from one of the disintegrators of the electrical ships. It swept through the crowded throng like a destroying blast. It was a panic of giants!

In the meantime the armed Martians outside the palace, hearing the uproar within, seeing our men pouring their fire through the windows, and supposing that we were guilty at once of treachery and assassination, had attempted an attack upon the electrical ships stationed round the building. But fortunately they had none of their larger engines at hand, and with their hand arms alone they had not been able to stand up against the disintegrators. They were blown away before the withering fire of the ships by the hundred until, fleeing from destruction, they rushed madly, driving their unarmed companions before them into the seething waters of the flood close at hand.

Chapter XVII

The Emperor Survives.

Through all this terrible contest the emperor of the Martians had remained standing upon his throne, gazing at the awful spectacle, and not moving from the spot. Neither he nor the frightened woman gathered upon the steps of the throne had been injured by the disintegrators. Their immunity was due to the fact that the position and elevation of the throne were such that it was not within the range of fire of the electrical ships which had poured their vibratory discharges through the windows, and we inside had only directed our fire toward the warriors who had attacked us.

Now that the struggle was over we turned our attention to Aina. Fortunately the girl had not been seriously injured and she was quickly restored to consciousness. Had she been killed, we would have been practically helpless in attempting further negotiations, because the knowledge which we had acquired of the language of the Martians from the prisoner captured on the golden asteroid, was not sufficient to meet the requirements of the occasion.

The Emperor Our Prisoner.

When the Martian monarch saw that we had ceased the work of death, he sank upon his throne. There he remained, leaning his chin upon his two hands and staring straight before him like that terrible doomed creature who fascinates the eyes of every beholder standing in the Sistine Chapel and gazing at Michael Angelo's dreadful painting of "The Last Judgement."

This wicked Martian also felt that he was in the grasp of pitiless and irresistible fate, and that a punishment too well deserved, and from which there was no possible escape, now confronted him.

There he remained in a hopelessness which almost compelled our sympathy, until Aina had so far recovered that she was once more able to act as our interpreter. Then we made short work of the negotiations. Speaking through Aina, the commander said:

"You know who we are. We have come from the earth, which, by your command, was laid waste. Our commission was not revenge, but self-protection. What we have done has been accomplished with that in view. You have just witnessed an example of our power, the exercise of which was not dictated by our wish, but compelled by the attack wantonly made upon a helpless member of our own race under our protection."

We Dictate Terms.

"We have laid waste your planet, but it is simply a just retribution for what you did with ours. We are prepared to complete the destruction, leaving not a living being in this world of yours, or to grant you peace, at your choice. Our condition of peace is simply this: 'All resistance must cease absolutely.'"

"Quite right," broke in Colonel Smith; "let the scorpion pull out his sting or we'll do it for him."

"Nothing that we could now do," continued the commander, "would in my opinion save you from ultimate destruction. The forces of nature which we have been compelled to let loose upon you will complete their own victory. But we do not wish, unnecessarily, to stain our hands further with your blood. We shall leave you in possession of your lives. Preserve them if you can. But, in case the flood recedes before you have all perished from starvation, remember that you here take an oath, solemnly binding yourself and your descendants forever never again to make war upon the earth."

We Show Mercy.

"That's really the best we can do," said Mr. Edison, turning to us. "We can't possibly murder these people in cold blood. The probability is that the flood has hopelessly ruined all their engines of war. I do not believe that there is one chance in ten that the waters will drain off in time to enable them to get at their stores of provisions before they have perished from starvation."

"It is my opinion," said Lord Kelvin, who had joined us (his pair of disintegrators hanging by his side, attached to a strap running over the back of his neck, very much as a farmer sometimes carries his big mittens), "it is my opinion that the flood will recede more rapidly than you think, and that the majority of these people will survive. But I quite agree with your merciful view of the matter. We must be guilty of no wanton destruction. Probably more than nine-tenths of the inhabitants of Mars have perished in the deluge. Even if all the others survived ages would elapse before they could regain the power to injure us."

The Martians Submit.

I need not describe in detail how our propositions were received by the Martian monarch. He knew, and his advisers, some of whom he had called in consultation, also knew, that everything was in our hands to do as we pleased. They readily agreed, therefore, that they would make no more resistance and that we and our electrical ships should be undisturbed while we remained upon Mars. The monarch took the oath prescribed after the manner of his race: thus the business was completed. But through it all there had been the shadow of a sneer on the emperor's face which I did not like. But I said nothing.

And now we began to think of our return home, and of the pleasure we should have in recounting our adventures to our friends on the earth, who were doubtless eagerly waiting for news from us. We knew they had been watching Mars with powerful telescopes, and we were also eager to learn how much they had seen and how much they had been able to guess of our proceedings.

But a day or two at least would be required to overhaul the electrical ships and to examine the state of our provisions. Those which we had brought from the earth, it will be remembered, had been spoiled and we had been compelled to replace them from the compressed provisions found in the Martians' storehouse. This compressed food had proved not only exceedingly agreeable to the taste, but very nourishing, and all of us had grown extremely fond of it. A new supply, however, would be needed in order to carry us back to the earth. At least sixty days would be required for the homeward journey, because we could hardly expect to start from Mars with the same initial velocity which we had been able to generate on leaving home.

In considering the matter of provisioning the fleet it finally became necessary to take an account of our losses. This was a thing that we had all shrunk from, because they had seemed to us almost too terrible to be borne. But now the facts had to be faced. Out of the 100 ships, carrying something more than two thousand souls, with which we had quitted the earth, there remained only fifty-five ships and 1,085 men! All the others had been lost in our terrific encounters with the Martians, and particularly in our first disastrous battle beneath the clouds.

Preparing to Return.

Among the lost were many men whose names were famous upon the earth, and whose death would be widely deplored when the news of it was received upon their native planet. Fortunately this number did not include any of those whom I have had occasion to mention in the course of this narrative. The venerable Lord Kelvin, who, notwithstanding his age, and his pacific disposition, proper to a man of science, had behaved with the courage and coolness of a veteran in every crisis; Monsieur Moissan, the eminent chemist; Prof. Sylvanus P. Thompson, and the Heidelberg Professor, to whom we all felt under special obligations because he had opened to our comprehension the charming lips of Aina—all these had survived, and were about to return with us to the earth.

It seemed to some of us almost heartless to deprive the Martians who still remained alive of any of the provisions which they themselves would require to tide them over the long period which must elapse before the recession of the flood should enable them to discover the sites of their ruined homes, and to find the means of sustenance. But necessity was now our only law. We learned from Aina that there must be stores of provisions in the neighborhood of the palace, because it was the custom of the Martians to lay up such stores during the harvest time in each Martian year in order to provide against the contingency of an extraordinary drought.

It was not with very good grace that the Martian Emperor acceded to our demands that one of the storehouses should be opened, but resistance was useless, and of course we had our way.

The supplies of water which we brought from the earth, owing to a peculiar process invented by Monsieur Moissan, had been kept in exceedingly good condition, but they were now running low and it became necessary to replenish them also. This was easily done from the Southern Ocean, for on Mars, since the levelling of the continental elevations, brought about many years ago, there is comparatively little salinity in the sea waters.

While these preparations were going on Lord Kelvin and the other men of science entered with the utmost eagerness upon those studies, the prosecution of which had been the principal inducement leading them to embark on the expedition. But, almost all of the face of the planet being covered with the flood, there was comparatively little that they could do. Much, however, could be learned with the aid of Aina from the Martians, now crowded on the land about the palace.

The results of these discoveries will in due time appear, fully elaborated in learned and authoritative treatises prepared by these savants themselves. I shall only call attention to one, which seemed to me very remarkable. I have already said that there were astonishing differences in the personal appearance of the Martians, evidently arising from differences of character and education, which had impressed themselves in the physical aspect of the individuals.

We now learned that these differences were more completely the result of education than we had at first supposed.

Looking about among the Martians by whom we were surrounded, it soon became easy for us to tell who were the soldiers and who were the civilians, simply by the appearance of their bodies, and particularly of their heads. All members of the military class resembled, to a greater or less extent, the monarch himself, in that those parts of their skulls which our phrenologists had designated as the bumps of destructiveness, combativeness and so on were enormously and disproportionately developed.

And all this, as we were assured, was completely under the control of the Martians themselves. They had learned, or invented, methods by which the brain itself could be manipulated, so to speak, and any desired portions of it could be specially developed, while the other parts of it were left to their normal growth. The consequence was that in the Martian schools and colleges there was no teaching in our sense of the word. It was all brain culture.

A Martian youth selected to be a soldier had his fighting faculties especially developed, together with those parts of the brain which impart courage and steadiness of nerve. He who was intended for scientific investigation had his brain developed into a mathematical machine, or an instrument of observation. Poets and literary men had their heads bulging with the imaginative faculties. The heads of inventors were developed into a still different shape.

"And so," said Aina, translating for us the words of a professor in the Imperial University of Mars, from whom we derived the greater part of our information on this subject, "the Martian boys do not study a subject; they do not have to learn it, but, when their brains have been sufficiently developed in the proper direction, they comprehend it instantly, by a kind of divine instinct."

But among the women of Mars, we saw none of these curious, and to our eyes monstrous, differences of development. While the men received, in addition to their special education, a broad general culture also, with the women there was no special education. It was all general in its character, yet thorough enough in that way. The consequence was that only female brains upon Mars were entirely well balanced. This was the reason why we invariably found the Martian women to be remarkably charming creatures, with none of those physical exaggerations and uncouth developments which disfigured their masculine companions.

All the books of the Martians, we ascertained, were books of history and of poetry. For scientific treatises they had no need, because, as I have explained, when the brains of those intended for scientific pursuits had been developed in the proper way the knowledge of nature's laws came to them without effort, as a spring bubbles from the rocks.

One word of explanation may be needed concerning the failure of the Martians, with all their marvellous powers, to invent electrical ships like those of Mr. Edison and engines of destruction comparable with our disintegrators. This failure was simply due to the fact that on Mars there did not exist the peculiar metals by the combination of which Mr. Edison had been able to effect his wonders. The theory involved in our inventions was perfectly understood by them, and had they possessed the means, doubtless they would have been able to carry it into practice even more effectively than we had done.

After two or three days all the preparations having been completed, the signal was given for our departure. The men of science were still unwilling to leave this strange world, but Mr. Edison decided that we could linger no longer.

At the moment of starting a most tragic event occurred. Our fleet was assembled around the palace, and the signal was given to rise slowly to a considerable height before imparting a great velocity to the electrical ships. As we slowly rose we saw the immense crowd of giants beneath us, with upturned faces, watching our departure. The Martian monarch and all his suite had come out upon the terrace of the palace to look at us. At a moment when he probably supposed himself to be unwatched he shook his fist at the retreating fleet. My eyes and those of several others in the flagship chanced to be fixed upon him. Just as he made the gesture one of the women of his suite, in her eagerness to watch us, apparently lost her balance and stumbled against him. Without a moment's hesitation, with a tremendous blow, he felled her like an ox at his feet.

A fearful oath broke from the lips of Colonel Smith, who was one of those looking on. It chanced that he stood near the principal disintegrator of the flagship. Before anybody could interfere he had sighted and discharged it. The entire force of the terrible engine, almost capable of destroying a fort, fell upon the Martian Emperor, and not merely blew him into a cloud of atoms, but opened a great cavity in the ground on the spot where he had stood.

A shout arose from the Martians, but they were too much astounded at what had occurred to make any hostile demonstrations, and, anyhow, they knew well that they were completely at our mercy.

Mr. Edison was on the point of rebuking Colonel Smith for what he had done, but Aina interposed.

"I am glad it was done," said she, "for now only can you be safe. That monster was more directly responsible than any other inhabitant of Mars for all the wickedness of which they have been guilty."

"The expedition against the earth was inspired solely by him. There is a tradition among the Martians—which my people, however, could never credit—that he possessed a kind of immortality. They declared that it was he who led the former expedition against the earth when my ancestors were brought away prisoners from their happy home, and that it was his image which they had set up in stone in the midst of the Land of Sand. He prolonged his existence, according to this legend, by drinking the waters of a wonderful fountain, the secret of whose precise location was known to him alone, but which was situated at that point where in your maps of Mars the name of the Fons Juventae occurs. He was personified wickedness, that I know; and he never would have kept his oath if power had returned to him again to injure the earth. In destroying him, you have made your victory secure."

Chapter XVIII

When at length we once more saw our native planet, with its well-remembered features of land and sea, rolling beneath our eyes, the feeling of joy that came over us transcended all powers of expression.

In order that all the nations which had united in sending out the expedition should have visual evidence of its triumphant return, it was decided to make the entire circuit of the earth before seeking our starting point and disembarking. Brief accounts in all known languages, telling the story of what we had done were accordingly prepared, and then we dropped down through the air until again we saw the well-loved blue dome over our heads, and found ourselves suspended directly above the white-topped cone of Fujiyama, the sacred mountain of Japan. Shifting our place toward the northeast, we hung above the city of Tokio and dropped down into the crowds that had assembled to watch us, the prepared accounts of our journey, which, the moment they had been read and comprehended, led to such an outburst of rejoicing as it would be quite impossible to describe.

One of the ships containing the Japanese members of the expedition dropped to the ground, and we left them in the midst of their rejoicing countrymen. Before we started—and we remained but a short time suspended above the Japanese capital—millions had assembled to greet us with their cheers.

We now repeated what we had done during our first examination of the surface of Mars. We simply remained suspended in the atmosphere, allowing the earth to turn beneath us. As Japan receded in the distance we found China beginning to appear. Shifting our position a little toward the south we again came to rest over the city of Pekin, where once more we parted with some of our companions, and where the outburst of universal rejoicing was repeated.

From Asia, crossing the Caspian Sea, we passed over Russia, visiting in turn Moscow and St. Petersburg.

Still the great globe rolled steadily beneath, and still we kept the sun with us. Now Germany appeared, and now Italy, and then

France, and England, as we shifted our position, first North then South, in order to give all the world the opportunity to see that its warriors had returned victorious from their far conquest. And in each country as it passed beneath our feet, we left some of the comrades who had shared our perils and our adventures.

At length the Atlantic had rolled away under us, and we saw the spires of the new New York.

The news of our coming had been flashed ahead from Europe, and our countrymen were prepared to welcome us. We had originally started, it will be remembered, at midnight, and now again as we approached the new capital of the world the curtain of night was just beginning to be drawn over it. But our signal lights were ablaze, and through these they were aware of our approach.

Again the air was filled with bursting rockets and shaken with the roar of cannon, and with volleying cheers, poured from millions of throats, as we came to rest directly above the city.

Three days after the landing of the fleet, and when the first enthusiasm of our reception had a little passed, I received a beautifully engraved card inviting me to be present in Trinity Church at the wedding of Aina and Sidney Phillips.

When I arrived at the church, which had been splendidly decorated, I found there Mr. Edison, Lord Kelvin, and all the other members of the crew of the flagship, and, considerably to my surprise, Colonel Smith, appropriately attired, and with a grace for the possession of which I had not given him credit, gave away the beautiful bride.

But Alonzo Jefferson Smith was a man and a soldier, every inch of him.

"I asked her for myself," he whispered to me after the ceremony, swallowing a great lump in his throat, "but she has had the desire of her heart. I am going back to the plains. I can get a command again, and I still know how to fight."

And thus was united, for all future time, the first stem of the Aryan race, which had been long lost, but not destroyed, with the latest offspring of that great family, and the link which had served to bring them together was the far-away planet of Mars.

Milton Keynes UK
Ingram Content Group UK Ltd.
UKHW030634140324
439439UK00006B/869